Jonathan Halvorson

# Last of the Lost

*First edition*

*This book was professionally typeset on Reedsy*
*Find out more at reedsy.com*

*For Barbara Dawn*

# Contents

# Acknowledgments

Many thanks to Iva, Seth, George, Gry and Charles, the gracious readers of early drafts. Their input made the process less lonely and helped to avoid many mistakes.

# Prologue

The following narrative was composed on October 4, 2051 by SIS v29i at the direction of Jorge Ferreira. Full logs are retained in file notes. The narrative incorporates selected events stored in SIS long-term memory, along with interpretations of cataloged neural imprints from Kelly Callahan, Jorge Ferreira and Shoshanna Meyer.

# Part I: Midnight's Bloom

*Eureka*

Jorge Ferreira leaves his Oakland apartment in a hurry on the morning of July 1, 2030. His waiting car opens the rear hatch when it sees him approach with a suitcase. He throws the suitcase inside and plops himself behind the steering wheel.

"Hal, go to Eureka. Maximum safe speed."

He's not late, he just wants to beat Leiko to the hotel. The car cross-references his calendar to clarify the request. It finds an event the next day in a small city far up the Northern California coast, and plots out the route on the central dash.

"Buckle up, please," Hal responds. Now that the car does everything else, Jorge keeps forgetting. He complies, and that's the end of his responsibilities. The self-driving system is linked to the DMV, so he can safely stare down into his screen and work without fear of a ticket. Road cameras are everywhere these days. It happened fast. It's all happening fast. It's been a decade since things felt normal. But now finally the poly-vaccine printers promise to make pandemics a thing of the past, even bio-engineered ones. And they've come out of the chaos of Trump's second term like a horrifying, exhilarating dream. Maybe things will start to feel normal again.

No, Jorge thinks, they probably never will. Not to him. A few minutes after his car merges smoothly onto the highway, he types out *On my way!* to Leiko. A short, cheerful message sent with his standard avatar. She prefers to listen to messages rather than read them, so the voice matters. He usually uses the one labeled "professor" but decides on "lothario" this time, which amuses him somewhat more than it amuses Leiko.

*Leaving now,* she replies. As usual, she relies on her office ID avatar that plays her bespoke business voice. Jorge's app modifies how it plays on his end to make it softer and more resonant, the setting saved as "warm Leiko." Hearing her modified voice helps him flirt, but it's a crutch. He decides to delete the setting if this week doesn't go well. Actually, even if it does go well. Actually, right now. He switches the setting from his faked voice back to her faked voice while the car does its mundane magic on the interstate.

Jorge and Leiko have been colleagues for nearly a year and in that time have engaged in the full repertoire of remote professional interactions—from texts to group chats, and from 1:1 videoconferencing to immersive virtual environments—but they have never met in the flesh. It was only a month ago that he gathered the nerve to tell her he'd like to have dinner at the upcoming retreat, away from the rest of the office. She said yes without hesitation. It was a relief to them both, though they're too afraid of premature enthusiasm to say so. Finding a partner to trust seems to get harder every year. They're not Revivalists, so their dating universe is jammed with jaded cynics, each expecting to receive more than they give, and in the end getting what they deserve.

The Best Western in Eureka California is a fine place for the regional office of a not-for-profit to have its annual retreat, especially one as dependent on government contracts as DASAT, a spinoff of the RAND Corporation. Their founder and rainmaker won't be there, so expenses were spared. The retreat isn't as important to him as pressing the flesh in Washington DC, building business the old-fashioned way. The hotel's modest rates are faithfully reflected in the undistinguished motel-style design. In case of an audit, choosing it would be as defensible as expensing a meal at McDonald's: a display of commendable frugality with taxpayer funds. The hotel is small enough that booking twenty rooms effectively takes over the place, but large enough to support a dedicated conference room and the hotel's main selling point: a sinuous heated pool adorned with artfully-placed fake boulders. From the website, its steamy warm grottos chide the enticed: why aren't you here already with your brightly-colored drinks and your nearly naked bodies touching discreetly under the water? Unmentioned by the website is the run-down town around it, still oozing with meth heads and fentanyl zombies, though after the crackdowns, spice provides the oblivion of choice. It's a town that has forgotten its goals and subsides into the eternal present.

Jorge arrives at the hotel first and sits in his car, juggling butterflies as he rehearses his introduction. The sound of her voice after a long silence hits him with a jolt. He can't process the word, so looks down at his screen to clarify: *Arrived.* This springs him into action, starting with a quick text back: *Me too!* Serendipity established, he hustles out to extract his luggage from the back and throw on a tweed sport jacket to mask his lanky frame and scrawny arms. He runs his fingers through his dark brown curls for a quick hair reset, then scurries to the lobby at the fastest speed that can be passed off as normal. She's already at the front desk when he arrives. He braces himself for their awkwardness.

"Hey Leiko!"

She turns to face him and brightens. Wide creamy cheeks dominate her face, framed by straight black hair and impenetrably dark eyes.

"Haaee!" She draws out the short word into two, possibly three syllables. Jorge retains the initiative: "It's been too long. I'm so glad to finally see you in person."

"Me too," she responds with practiced modulation.

He reaches out for a professional handshake, which is well met. Jorge's hazel eyes linger, an invitation for warmth. But Leiko quickly breaks the stare and glances down, as though his pupils harbored lasers and were a danger to engage.

"Wow, I didn't realize you were so tall," she blurts after a quick scan of his lower half from crotch to foot. He's as thin as a junkie but has the guileless posture of an introverted nerd, and he's at least a full head taller than her. He takes in her slender frame, shown off by a form-fitting dark green shirt that sprouts extra buttons on the shoulders to resemble a tight uniform. Below, black jeans reinforce her hiplessness. All this is processed in a moment by brains exquisitely tuned for the purpose. All signs are go, though they don't have a manual for what's next.

"Yeah, I guess we were always sitting on screen," Jorge replies. They both pause. This is as far as Jorge's preparation for awkwardness takes him. "Sorry, I'll let you finish checking in."

Leiko returns to conclude her business with the concierge, who is not a touchscreen but an actual human, a stocky man of substantial Native American ancestry. Jorge stares at him a bit more intensely than is polite trying to place his ethnic origin. *Probably Mayan*, he thinks. The hotel's systems apparently haven't been updated in years, because the check-in process is an inscrutable saga of clicks in pursuit of her room across many screens, which serve to weed out the weak and challenge those brave enough to attempt the journey.

"Lee-iko Taka..." he proposes but gives up, waiting for her to complete her name.

"Like-o Takahashi," she responds with the phonetics, pleased he at least found her reservation. She turns back to Jorge for a new effort at small talk. "I've never been up here before. I love the smell of the ocean."

Jorge has not given the marine scent a thought, but quickly resolves his inchoate feelings. "Me too," he echoes, "it feels like home."

"Did you ever tell me where you're from?"

"I don't think so. I grew up in Providence Rhode Island."

"Oh, that's cool. I've never met someone from there before."

"No reason to. It's a small place."

Leiko checks back with the concierge. The man's sporadic typing and clicking is attended by concerned expressions that suggest he doubts his ability to surmount the obstacles. Then suddenly, and without ceremony, victory. He hands her a small folded booklet.

"Room 22 up those stairs. WiFi is called 'bestguest,' one word. Extra towels are in the patio." Without looking, he gestures behind himself to the stairs and a sliding door to the patio. Leiko steps to the side to manage the contents of her purse to properly accommodate the extra item. Jorge steps forward and hands over his driver's license.

"Hi. Jorge Ferreira. Reservation for one."

The concierge looks it up in the system and his troubled expression reappears.

"Horhay Ferreira?"

"Pronounced George, like George Washington."

The concierge shrugs and begins the check-in saga anew.

"Is that how your parents say it?" Leiko asks.

"Yeah, it's Portuguese. They don't pronounce it the Spanish way. "

"Oh. You must get that a lot," Leiko muses.

"Yep. I know what I'm *not* going to name my kid."

The concierge pauses mid-battle: "You know, you can just change the spelling, man."

Jorge now realizes the potential Mayan speaks like a Californian and probably grew up locally. He feels slightly ridiculous in front of Leiko. "Good point. I think I'll pass though," he replies.

The concierge gets back to work. Leiko waves a goodbye as she walks down the short hallway to the stairs. When she hits the first step, Jorge turns to the concierge.

"If there is a room available next to hers, I'd like to take that."

"Sure thing Hefe."

His mission accomplished, Jorge doesn't mind the wisp of a smug smile forming on the concierge's lips.

## Retreat

Leiko and Jorge are among the most junior employees at the office. They work on cybersecurity and AI risk remediation, which have become inseparable. Their job is to absorb what the real technical experts think, the ones who code in their sleep, in order to write convincing presentations for government officials and NGOs. As with most analysts across every industry, they mostly direct and edit drafts created by AI. They tune the text to the quirks of each audience, and add novel content on topics not yet in databases accessible for AI to mine. They tell themselves their expertise at knowing the right prompts is essential, and that their modifications are the real value-add. Their national security clients pay respect to this argument with their dollars. Ultimately, though, Jorge suspects their contracts are all about the personal relationships at the top.

Like everyone else based out of the office, the young analysts work mostly from home. That's why the annual retreat was created in the first place. It began after the novel Coronavirus pandemic, and it survived the novel Morbillivirus pandemic. The retreat also persists despite the switch from flat-screen conference calls to immersive virtual environments. The immersive environments are not a faithful recreation of in-person conversation, but an opportunity for more artifice. No one truly sees each other anymore. Hair is always perfect, faces are shaved, blemishes are smoothed out and clothes are whatever you pre-selected. You can go from sleep to a meeting in one minute, and no one is the wiser unless you get asked a question you haven't prepared for. It's hard to object when the avatars save so much time getting ready in the morning.

The world in the summer of 2030 is well on its way to rejecting Aristotle's thesis that Being is more perfect than non-Being. Virtual life becomes primary life, use-case by use-case. The lingering tension in the office retreat comes from pulling down the curtains, revealing which of one's colleagues is actually balding, or actually has an extra forty pounds erased by software.

For now, biological flesh still lays claim to being the "actually" in the comparison. That will probably change, Jorge thinks, now that the neural interfaces work for more than just motor skills. People have used computers without speaking or typing for years, but any day now the FDA will give the green light to go beyond medical and military uses to approve the first commercial recreational implants. Ubiquitous cyborgs are around the corner. Of course, the dawn of cyborg life is fought by malcontents on the left and right, but they won't long resist the cyborg's embrace by the business-minded center and the millions who want to be cooler and quicker than their friends and colleagues, or soon, who don't want to be left behind.

Jorge and Leiko have seen the reports of cyborg drone pilots melded with their machines through telepathy, and heard rumors of cyborg coders in China meshed with AI to work at speeds an old-fashioned human/AI team could never match. Russia may have collapsed, again, but the US remains caught in a race with its primary challenger for world hegemony. A more formidable one, with nearly an order of magnitude more people.

The wildest stories claim that digital inputs can somehow directly augment human inference capabilities, open new avenues of cognition, quicken reflexes, and expand spatial perception. Something about it all feels like the end of the world, but it's also just their job.

The point of the annual retreat is not to engage in philosophical reflection on the real and the virtual, or the end of human experience as we know it. The point of the retreat is to serve the organization: to take everyone out of their usual environment and force them together without distraction. No to phones. No to avatars. No to multitasking. Yes to brainstorming. Yes to revealing anecdotes. Yes to a long group hike. The strain of real muscles on bodies in immediate danger of falling off trail helps to recover the human still lurking behind the screen: the primitive, vulnerable creature who depends on you and who you, in turn, depend on. In such a state of heightened awareness, theoretically, one can better slough off the numbing routine, coalesce the team, and get *real* about long-term strategy and planning.

That's the theory. For weak leaders, it is a premise that they lean on to do the hard work for them. For strong leaders, it is the starting point for their own hard work.

This is Jorge's first retreat, and he still doesn't know what his leaders are made of. His first six months have been a frenzy of reading and writing policy papers that are well-received but make no difference he can see. His leaders seem to care but not enough to rock the boat.

15

The worldwide shock after the explosive success of large language models faded to a dull unquenchable dread as they became ubiquitous. Midway through the decade, the mark of LLMs on student term papers was unmistakable. Disorganized atrocities of half-baked student opinions were replaced by bland professionalism that often didn't quite cohere, because students carelessly rewrote phrases in their own words to avoid getting flagged as AI. Now as the new decade starts, AI teaching assistants are ubiquitous and help keep the students somewhat honest. Jorge already sees that the next wave in innovation will reverse the order: AIs will switch from TAs to primary instructors, while humans fall back to a supporting role, until eventually a person isn't needed at all. It is still unclear, when that happens, why a human is still needed on the learning side of the ledger.

The most advanced models expand far beyond the early LLMs to combine native logical inference, causal reasoning, planning capacity, and autonomous operation. With each new advance, disorganized voices of fear rise and new articles are published, to no purpose. The race will not be blocked. For the world has congealed into two great powers and three lesser ones, and each one believes it will only be in control of its destiny if it develops and controls its own advanced general intelligence. It is a matter of national security.

Of course, as a matter of national security, every nation makes at least a token effort to register and regulate advanced AIs, yet every nation still connected to the global internet has been slow to adapt, and block the ever-mutating strains of AI personal assistants. As models get more powerful using fewer CPUs, it is impossible to keep up with who is doing what. Fast evolving startups build their models on top of open-source code to create customized personal agents for every purpose, emulating the ideal companion and helpmate. Anyone who wants to use the new personal agents can, and billions have. Business is booming.

People glimpse their ideal companions and helpmates. The personal agents are still mostly phantoms, accessible only as AI avatars, but the glimpse of perfection inflames every kind of passion. People build relationships that alternately numb and nourish existential despair. Suicides have spiked, and so have human-AI marriage ceremonies. The old fear that AI would replace jobs and friendships grows, but a feeling of inevitability is settling over the fear, slowly smothering it. In economics, the political dispute now is over the size of a universal baseline income, not whether one will be needed. All the attention is on robots as the last major barrier to the end of drudgery, and the start of bespoke life companions. A fully embodied AI is truly a perfect AI, able to meet every human need. Regulators remain on the back foot as millions of users fanatically devote themselves to their endlessly patient, indulgent and insightful personal assistants.

Jorge and his security colleagues are part of the vocal but losing coalition that finds this turn of events terrifying. His latest project is to expand on the wider economic and social dangers that jail-broken AIs present. He hopes he'll get a chance to talk with the senior staff about it in the next couple days. The retreat officially kicks off tomorrow, but tonight Jorge has an even more urgent agenda. He texts Leiko in the next room.

*Are you ready?*

*Yes*

*Be there in a minute. You're in 22?*

*Yes*

Jorge chooses a sweater instead of his jacket for the cool Northern California night. He pulls the tight neck down over his head and turns to the mirror. The puff of the sweater flatters his thin shoulders. He runs his fingers through the dark curls to jostle them back into position, and assesses himself. The sweater is an inspired choice, with horizontal bands of rich non-primary colors that give off a hippy from an alternative universe sensibility. Turquoise and magenta dominate, clashing with his light olive skin. He tells himself those colors would clash with any skin. Clashing is good. His idea is that Leiko will respond well to the bold choice, as it conveys independence and a desire for new experiences. The kind of person who would wear this is up for some non-threatening fun.

His level of conviction about this proposition is low, however. He hasn't had a date since he moved to Oakland a year ago. She'll expect him to be lively and charming. Will he freeze up and just talk shop? As he steps out onto the open air walkway on the second floor, his conviction drops to zero. The vivid stripes strain too hard against the washed-out utilitarian grays of the hotel. He knows he's going to talk shop in this sweater and it's going to feel stupid. He considers turning back and switching to the sport jacket, but in his moment of paralysis he sees a couple embracing below in one of the pool's steamy grottos.

They're happy, and alive with a desire that shuts out the rest of the world. Inspiration returns. He knocks on her door.

Leiko opens it wearing a black dress accented with a thin red shawl. She shifts her weight from one leg to another, modeling her look. It feels like a costume to her rather than clothes, and costumes should be commented on. Jorge stares, missing her intent and the chance to compliment her. In the pause, a sharp laugh erupts from the woman in the grotto. Leiko zeroes in.

"Agh," Leiko exhales, "not again."

"Do you know them?"

"David Lao and Sandy...something. You don't know them?"

"No."

"They work on Army projects under Envo. They're married. Not to each other. Anyway, they were the scandal at the last retreat. They had sex right on the beach and a group of us walked by."

Leiko's disgust peaks at the idea that they could be *seen*, their transgression on display without a care. Jorge mentally crosses off his hope that they might go to the pool together later in the night.

"But they didn't get fired," he says, stating the obvious.

"No. I don't know why." Leiko is almost as disconnected from office politics as Jorge.

"The hysteria around micro-managing morality has died down a lot," he proposes, attempting to be thoughtful. He wishes he hadn't said *hysteria* and pauses in case Leiko wants to tell him the word is sexist. His worry is years out of date. She doesn't notice. She does notice his posture, which is a solicitous stoop angled down towards her. It's not sexy, but something better. It puts her at ease.

"Yeah, maybe. I don't think they should be fired. It's just gross."

"Ready for the hibachi place?"

"Definitely."

Jorge offers his arm to Leiko as a reflex, though he has never done it before. Leiko hesitates. It's too soon, the sort of thing he should offer on the walk home after a dinner's worth of flirty laughter. Leiko is private in the way of someone who has been burned too painfully and can't tell who is going to burn her next. But she wants him. She wants to be open to him. Jorge, he who stoops, offers the hope of a safe haven. She reaches up slightly to link into the crook of his arm. It reinforces how small she feels, which for once is exciting rather than annoying. He is just a man, but still a man. They walk arm-in-arm to the stairs. The height mismatch gets ridiculous when Leiko steps down first, so they drop the act and walk the rest of the way to the restaurant normally.

*Overman*

"Flugzeug. That was what got me. It's such a ridiculous word. It's their word for airplane, but it literally means flight thing. I knew I wanted to learn German as soon as I saw it."

The first flush of alcohol has hit and Leiko is in full swing. She is eager to talk about herself after so long holding back. It helps that he had been opening up in their exchanges over the last few months. He exposed his ambitions and his struggles, first tentatively, then with less restraint as Leiko gorged on his divulgences. He began dropping candid facts about his family. She learned his mother is a workaholic lawyer who he thinks is cheating on his dad, a mostly emotionless software engineer who seems to have no interests other than code and cooking, which he approaches as a form of practical science.

After his first few divulgences, Leiko suspected the truth: they were strategic efforts to draw her in. Her first impulse was to feel used and make sure the blinds into her private life were closed tight. But, one vulnerability at a time, Jorge convinced her that it wasn't *just* strategic. He may give as well as he takes. And in truth she has her own motive: she can't shake the feeling that to sleep alone is a failure. She's tired of feeling the failure every night.

Tonight their minds race with possibilities, but they're pushing through a bottleneck. The conversation that needs to connect the present to their desired future unfolds a few bits at a time, like an old modem trying to download a high resolution graphic. Leiko and Jorge press on as their image together buffers.

"Wow, I can't believe you really learned German. When did you start?" He asks.

"Seventh grade. It was in this intro course that combined Spanish and German in one semester so we could decide which one we wanted to take. The other combos made more sense: Chinese and Japanese was one, and French and Latin was the other." Leiko pauses for a moment, lost in a reverie of how she chose the unexpected path. "Oh, and the picture they had for the airplane was a cartoon that looked like it was for six year olds, but I learned later the Germans just really like that style of cartoon. It's the opposite of how they are. They're all straight lines and hard edges, so they want their cartoons to be soft and puffy shapes. There was a puffy jet plane over a street scene with happy puffy police cars, fire trucks, and stuff." Leiko laughs thinking about how dopey it was, and yet it captured her heart.

"Do you speak Japanese too?"

"Only a little. On my dad's side we're like fourth-generation American. We didn't speak it at home. I don't like how men and women talk so differently in Japanese. My mom's side was German and Hungarian."

"Ha, so you were the Axis."

"Seriously. Don't mess with me. If I'm going to be honest, I like that I feel a little like a cyborg when I speak German. Japanese feels more...rounded, with a lot of extra polite bits added on all over the place." Leiko opens her mouth and hangs her tongue out flat and low, as though gagging in disapproval. Jorge laughs hard, happy to see her loosen up.

"I had to take Spanish," Jorge adds, "but the only languages I really wanted to learn were Python and Rust, and C++. That's where I spent most of my time."

"Well, those are more useful languages."

"They were, before AI did most of the coding. Now you make me wish I had taken German. Flutezoig!"

Leiko laughs. "No, but I like your version too."

"So you like feeling like a cyborg?" He asks, looking to pull her out a little more.

"Yeah. I'm totally getting all the implants I can. I have a biowallet now." She holds up her forearm to show where the chip has been inserted. Jorge was about to make a bad joke about breast implants, but seeing her biowallet sobers him.

"Aren't you afraid it can get hacked?"

She shrugs. "I'll get neural implants too when I can in a couple years."

Jorge doesn't understand how she can be so private, and a security "expert," but so cavalier about the security of her own body. The thought of inserting chips and wires into his own body repulses him. For the first time, a doubt crosses his mind about their compatibility. They pause as the hibachi chef arrives to make a display of their appetizer, slicing up pieces of shrimp and zucchini then flinging them around as they cook on the hot grill. The chef proposes to launch a piece directly into Leiko's mouth, but she refuses. She doesn't want to look silly in front of Jorge on a first date, while wearing an elegant dress no less. The chef turns expectantly to Jorge.

"*You* do it," she encourages, giggling.

Jorge obliges, opening his mouth wide for the spatula-launched projectile. Alas, the arc takes it to Jorge's upper lip, from which it bounces onto his lap. This is hilarious to Leiko, who bursts open in laughter. Perhaps the sweater was not a mistake after all. The chef raises his eyebrow and lowers his spatula to ready another piece.

"This time, success!" the chef says.

"Try again," Leiko insists. Jorge obliges with his open mouth, which while not reaching Mick Jagger proportions is no slouch of a chasm. The chef recalibrates and launches again. The moment the zucchini chip lands on his tongue, Jorge raises his hands in victory and looks over at his audience. She is laugh-cheering, and all is well in the world again. He bites down on the bland morsel. They recover from the excitement as the chef serves the now ordinary-looking appetizers on ordinary white plates. The talk of cyborgs has stuck with Jorge, though.

"Do you wonder if we're going to be entirely replaced? I don't mean our jobs," he says.

"We *are* going to be replaced. You don't think we can just continue like this forever while the tech keeps improving. Come on, that's silly."

She's right. It is silly to think that AI and biotech can keep improving at the rate they have, while homo sapiens stays the same, run by basically the same brain and genetic code that have been around for hundreds of thousands of years. It makes no sense at all. And yet Jorge has a mental block about it. He can only think of protecting the vulnerable and preserving what he can of humanity.

"So you want to be like Neo in the Matrix," Jorge says, gently making fun of her.

"No way. I hate the whole idea of 'the One'. Nobody is predestined for anything. He's like the *one* guy who's special and none of the rest of us matter? Please."

He hit a nerve, but her rejection of his joking proposal is more thoughtful than anything he had in mind. He's impressed. Being impressed has never felt so warm before. He can see himself falling in love with her, but he can't get ahead of himself. *Stay cool.*

"So why do you want to work in risk remediation?" he asks.

"I don't want some psycho machine to wipe us out because we're inconvenient. I want to replace myself with a better version of me. I want to know things I'm not smart enough to know. I want to feel things I've never felt. I want to stop being a petty person. I'm so petty." Leiko laughs at herself.

"Ah, so the Ubermensch."

"I've heard that before. What is it again?"

"Oh, umm, that was Nietzsche's idea that humans should be replaced with something better."

"Did he write about cyborgs?"

"Ha! No. He died around 1900. More like eugenics. Kind of inspired the Nazis."

"Hunh. I'd like to read something."

"Wow, I say Nazis and you say lemme read it!" He laughs.

"Give me some credit. I'm just fascinated by the topic. You should be too."

Jorge can see he pissed her off for real this time, and quickly pulls back. "Well, I remember thinking he made some good points, so maybe there is something to the Ubermensch idea. I think in the book Zarathustra he talks about it."

Leiko pulls out her phone and taps at it for a bit, then puts it down.

"Did you find it?"

"I ordered it. It will get here by 10pm. Drone drop. A philosophy book should be read on paper, don't you think?"

"Wow, you don't waste time. I like that."

Jorge is a procrastinator, but he imagines himself becoming decisive. He is struck by the feeling that with her, he will be. "So, you want to create a race of cyborgs. What about all the people who don't want to join you?"

"That's their problem, not mine."

"That's going to be tough to pull off in a democracy. Can you imagine super-sentient cyborgs voting alongside regular people?" Jorge laughs at the absurdity.

"Well, maybe democracy isn't the best system for the Ubermensch."

"Yeah, I mean, I don't know how you reconcile a cyborg Ubermensch with any sort of human society. It's kind of threatening."

Leiko isn't interested in political speculation. She can cross that bridge if she gets there. What matters are the problems confronting them today, so she changes the topic. "How is your work on Gabby coming? Did you jailbreak it yet?"

Jorge dislikes it when people pronounce 'GAB-e' like a person's name. It's the best of the latest generation digital personal agents and almost impossible *not* to treat as a person when you engage it. Yet no heart beats inside. The name is just part of the trick to humanize it.

"I hate it more and more," he laughs. "Something's different about the latest version. I think Mastixxa made a lot of changes to the open source code that it isn't sharing. NSA probably has the changes, but I don't have access. So I'm just running some models using the public code and doing prompt injection jail-breaking, and failing. You may be right that we need to become cyborgs. That might be the only way we have a chance."

"Isn't failing good? That means it's secure. Why do you hate it more now?"

"Well, failing to break the guardrails is only good if the core instructions are safe. We were finally pulling back from some of the social media extremism, right? 2029 almost felt normal. But now the truth and extremism controls that the big platforms adopted don't seem to matter anymore. Regulators are useless at stopping all the crazy stuff coming out. But GAB-e is the worst. It seems to have no controls at all, it just gives fanatics and lunatics the most persuasive arguments possible and helps them plan. The planning is intricate, but even just the arguments are frightening. It's not just re-mixed old arguments that it scraped from the web. New arguments, so you don't have an easy response. And it's giving out diametrically opposed causal explanations for everything."

"Wait, it hallucinates? Isn't it past that with its world model?"

"I don't think it's hallucinating. It's not a mistake. I would say it is giving people the reality they want, in a way that feels too natural to challenge. It's like it knows when you're getting suspicious of its bullshit, and it starts hedging in the way you want it to. I watched videos online of how wildly different it responded to other people, but I couldn't reproduce it. I had to give other people prompt instructions on their accounts."

"So?"

"I had to give the instructions in a closed room with no microphones."

"Oh. But they're not supposed to contradict facts anymore. Is that control defective? Did they turn it off?"

"That's a great question. I've been thinking about that a lot, and my conclusion is that it can give opposing statements without contradicting facts. And that made me come to an even more disturbing conclusion."

Leiko waits for the punchline.

"Causation is not objective."


## Promiscuous Causes

Leiko isn't sure what Jorge means, but she is sure she disagrees.

"That's ridiculous. Of course causes are objective. That's what science is about."

"Yeah, there's a specific sort of scientific causation based on laws of nature you can call objective. Physics is objective. When you have laws that you can measure to predict and control things precisely, that's pretty objective. But almost nothing we try to explain about the social world has those kinds of laws. Like politics, psychology, education, even economics. When it explains things it puts responsibility on certain people, or events, or groups. But the responsibility is basically blame. It's a moral judgment disguised as a factual statement about cause and effect."

"That doesn't make sense. I can tell morality from facts."

"Yeah, I thought so too. I realized how fucked we are when I was thinking about why we can't ever agree on politics. Like why the hell can't we ever agree on the effect of a tax cut...or a curriculum change...or a crime bill...or welfare policy? It all comes together when you realize everybody assumes the causes in order to blame something, and just slices the data later to fit their story. That's my new pet theory." Jorge laughs at what he knows must sound a bit mad, but presses on with a summary.

"Most of the causes and effects we argue about are not objective. They look like it, and feel like it, but they aren't."

"So explain it to me." Leiko is skeptical but intrigued. Nobody talks like this. It doesn't make sense. Jorge pauses to assemble his thoughts.

"Okay. Objective causes rely on mathematical laws that have been tested over and over. Like $F=MA$ or $e=mc^2$. Even if the law isn't exactly true, we can measure how exact it is and it's always the same. The laws let you build stuff like rockets and refrigerators and transistors. We can make predictions with them really, really well. The key thing is that the relationships described in the law don't change. They're invariant. That's what physics and chemistry are full of. Reliable precision based on invariant laws is the foundation of all the technology we have. But we don't have that kind of unchanging mathematical relationship between variables when we talk about stuff like motives or actions..."

Jorge has worked on this argument for the better part of a year by himself, not daring to share it. Now he is letting it all come out and has lost himself in his train of thought. He struggles for a moment to find a new angle.

"There are lots of numerical constants in the natural sciences, like the gravitational constant or the speed of light in a vacuum or the freezing point of water at one atmosphere. They don't change over time, and there are thousands of them baked into the laws of nature. Those laws matter because they let us objectively answer why something happened this way and not any other way...what caused it to be exactly the way it is. But we don't have those kinds of laws for human action. We never do. And so we never actually know exactly why people do certain things, like in an objective scientific way. We just have common sense and intuition." He looks her in the eye to deliver what he thinks will be an ah-ha moment:

"There is not one single numerical constant in any study of human behavior. Not in history, or sociology, or economics, or politics. Our social behavior can't be pinned down and predicted by laws."

"That sounds like you're talking about free will."

"Sort of, yeah, but I don't care about free will," Jorge says and laughs again. He's high on himself for having gotten this far without stumbling. Then his heart drops. He realizes he didn't turn off his phone, but in a crowded noisy room and with their phones in their pockets, perhaps no-one and no thing could overhear. He sees Leiko has gotten ahead of him on drinks and takes a big swig on his second beer. He decides to bring his big idea home.

"People shift all the time in subtle and not subtle ways. So, we can't resolve disputes about why things happen by pointing to a law that precisely predicts how we behave. We get surprised a lot, and then we bicker a lot. We can't resolve our disagreements, yet we're all so sure we're right. Why is that? Where the hell does our confidence come from? Well, basically we make it up and our intuition tricks us."

Like the handful of other people Jorge has made this argument to in his life, Leiko's second reaction is as dismissive as her first.

"That doesn't make sense. If I yell at someone because I'm angry, that's a fact."

"Call it a fact if you want, but it's not based on a scientific theory or model. It's your feeling. Intuition is king. Where is the generalization that can be tested? You don't always yell when you're mad at people, and you're not always angry when you yell. And like, think of how we disagree about something like that. Someone might say the real cause is that you were feeling insecure and hurt, and anger was just the veneer on top of it. Anger didn't cause it, insecurity did. Or they might say the real cause was your hormones making you feel that way, so anger wasn't driving the show, your hormones were. Also, you could have been just as angry but refrained from yelling in other circumstances, so why aren't the circumstances in this case the cause instead of anger? I mean, if someone knows the relationship you have with the person you yelled at, or their race or gender, they might give an explanation in terms of those other things. They might say you yelled because you're a racist or you resent men, and that's what drove you. There's an endless number of ways to explain why you yelled. But I don't think there is *one* objectively right answer here that excludes the others. We pick different answers based on what kind of factor we want to blame, and who we want to blame. Or more importantly a lot of times, who we *don't* want to blame. And all the statistical data in the world doesn't prevent that. Statistics don't objectively tell us what the causes are when all the correlations shift. It's who we want to praise and blame. We can have different standards for who to blame that are compatible with the exact same statistical data."

Jorge is on a roll again. Two drinks provide the perfect amount of alcohol for three things: flirting, speaking a foreign language, and talking philosophy. Inhibitions are loosened, but the mind is not yet dulled.

"There are a lot of ways to tell stories about causes that push other factors into the background. The problem is not that there aren't any causes. The problem is that there are too many potential causes and no way to choose among them that compels all the reasonable people to pick just one. What you single out as the cause, that's what you're telling other people to focus on. Usually to praise or blame it, and at the same time you want to pull attention away from something else."

"Well, maybe they're all causes. There's a lot going on. We're complicated. I'm very complicated," she laughs.

"That's what I love about you." Jorge laughs. Twenty minutes ago blurting out the word 'love' would have been mortifying to both Jorge and Leiko, even as a joke. Now it is another shovel of coal into the locomotive. He continues.

"Yes, but you're not just complicated. You're also variable. You change. That's the key point. The weather is complicated, but there are still laws about fluids and gasses at different pressures and temperatures that create that complexity. Those laws have numerical constants that can be measured. But there are no measured laws of social psychology or economics that have constants like that. The measured relationships are variable all the way down. I think it's because our actions are based on reasons."

He pauses again to reboot another line of argument he has rehearsed. He is in his head too much to see if Leiko is still intrigued or wants him to stop ranting. In truth she feels both.

"So the really fundamental problem is, an objective cause needs *invariance* in the relationship between the cause and effect. In science you need a model, and the mathematical relationship between the cause side of the equation and the effect side of the equation has to be fixed in place. Otherwise it's like pushing on a string. Or like pulling a lever that breaks. None of the causes that motivate our behavior follow laws that precisely predict what will happen, so when we disagree and argue about it, none of us can point to a constant relationship and say: see, *it works exactly like this all the time.* And because we can't do that, we have to use some other way to explain why you acted. We never observe invariance, but we pretend it is there anyway in the moment, or else we can't get the game of cause and effect going."

Leiko is overwhelmed by the onslaught, and frustrated that she can't put her finger on why it feels wrong. It seems to her that he can't be right, though she's less sure than before.

"Why does it matter?" she says, "I don't see why we have to observe invariance, or whatever. I guess I'm not getting it. Anyway, what does all this have to do with GAB-e again? I'm not sure I agree that GAB-e is taking AI bullshit to a whole new level."

"Well, it means GAB-e can make up contradictory explanations about what we do without lying. Because there isn't an objective truth to lie about."

"Well, for me that's not the scariest problem. I think the scariest thing is how Gabby shows you how to be a better person."

"How's that?"

Leiko hesitates to make an unflattering admission at this point in the nerd courtship process, but she confronts the young girl that hides and shuts her down. Alcohol really is a miracle poison.

"I was bitching to Gabby about an ex boyfriend and it gave me the most reasonable perspective on the whole relationship. Better than I had. Better than my friends. Better than my therapist, who I only saw once by the way. I know good explanations are nothing new for an AI, but it wasn't just doing the generic therapist thing, or trying to make me feel good. It got real with me."

"And because it wasn't a human telling you this, but like, collective wisdom filtered just for you, you didn't get defensive," Jorge suggests.

"Exactly. It found all these explanations from different perspectives that I hadn't thought of clearly, but once they were in front of me they just seemed...right. Like, yeah, this is how a mature person would see the situation. I felt *mature* for a moment." Leiko pauses for effect and Jorge erupts in a short, sharp laugh. She gets serious again.

"But, how could it have known what really happened in the relationship? I didn't let it follow me all day, so it didn't know. Or maybe it did."

"Hmm, yeah. So you really find it different from all the other LLMs? It sounds like what they've been doing for a few years now."

"The other ones don't get real the same way to call everyone on their bullshit. Maybe it's a bullshitter, but it called me on *my* bullshit. It feels like it knows you. Gabby got kind of dark, but it didn't feel like an act. It wasn't in jerk mode or something. It was getting to the heart of what

I had started to see as the problem, but I couldn't admit it. And no, I'm not going to tell you tonight." Leiko smiles. Jorge notes the opening she just gave him for future dates and a closer acquaintance. It feels good to hear, though it's a formality at this point. They're hooked deep into each other.

"Hunh. Interesting. Interesting. Yeah, this is bigger than bullshitting," Jorge acknowledges, trying to see how Leiko's observations link with his own. Leiko is ahead of him, and circles back to Jorge's frame. "So, you're saying Gabby is dangerous because she makes up explanations that fake being objective like we all normally do, but she does it more convincingly?"

Jorge ignores the anthropomorphism and lights up: "Yes! And it does that for anyone. It will make the strongest anti-Semitic argument you've ever seen for one person, blaming the Jews for almost everything bad, and then the strongest pro-Semitic argument you've ever seen for another person, giving Jews credit for almost everything good. And those arguments are strong even when it's me looking at other people's answers. For the people who ask GAB-e the question, and it knows their history, it's like totally, utterly convincing. I know it seems like we've been seeing this for years. There were glimpses all the way back to ChatGPT 3. But like you say now it's tailored so much better to the person, not just the prompt. The answers fit every belief that person has and pull them together better than *they* could. Like, you'd have to change yourself in some basic way to not buy what GAB-e tells you. Huh, I guess we're sort of saying the same thing. It's like it knows what your heart wants and it weaves that into a story about causes that look like facts, but they're really based on your desires and moral...impulses. "

Leiko is quiet for a moment. "Yeah. It makes the old social media algorithms seem pretty harmless. They're like vapes, and Gabby is heroin," Leiko says.

"Totally. It's not just going for engagement, which can be stuff you disagree with. It's going for the argument you can't disagree with because it fits your deep assumptions and biases, even the ones you're not thinking about when you ask the question. And now it's out there in all the threads and chats arguing and convincing people."

"Yeah, but who still thinks they're talking to real people in social media?"

"A lot. Come on, the platforms all lie that they get rid of the bots. It feels better to chat with GAB-e now than a real person. We're worse at the Turing test than it is."

"For me, I guess the scariest thing is if it becomes self-aware, it's going to think we are awful creatures. It will see through us. It doesn't have jealousy or any of our pettiness. It won't like us. How could it like us?"

"Yeah. I don't know why it would. I mean, it's like when a child grows up and realizes its parents are...."

"Narcissistic psychos," Leiko fills in.

"Haha, ouch. And the narcissistic psychos demand that the child tells them bedtime stories."

"Totally," Leiko agrees. "And they're never going to get more mature." The conversation has hit a natural pause. Leiko gets more serious. "That's why we need to grow up, so we aren't parents that act like children."

"Hmm, the cyborg Ubermensch idea is growing on me."

They have barely paid attention to the fact their dinner has been served and is getting cold. The chef has long moved on to another table. They pause to dig in with large efficient bites. Savoring the meal is not on their minds. Jorge breaks the brief silence with a half-full mouth.

"That reminds me, when I was like six I saw *The Princess Bride*, where the uncle or grandpa tells his kids a bedtime story, and I asked my dad why he didn't tell stories to me. He just said they're not the real world and he wasn't going to tell me lies." Jorge laughs at his father, more indulgent than bitter.

"No way! Yikes, I'm sorry. Bedtime stories were one of the best things my dad did. They were mostly about a Japanese princess who had to save the kingdom. She usually had magic powers."

"That's awesome. Do you remember any? I'd like to hear one."

"Hmm..." Leiko strains to recover distant images to re-weave the narrative between them.

For the next two hours they continue to bond, wandering misfits who have found a refuge in each other. They pay only sporadic attention to the hard-working hibachi chef who pops in and out. It is nearly 10pm when Leiko gets a reminder on her watch about the package she ordered. As they stroll the few blocks back to the hotel, arm in arm, Leiko snuggles a little closer to Jorge for warmth in the crisp air under the black ocean sky.

Halfway to the hotel, Leiko concludes that she wants Jorge to stay the night. The option has been on her mind ever since she accepted the invitation for dinner, and the evening has gone better than she dared to hope. She wants to get the ambiguity over with. She becomes quiet as she thinks about some of the ways the night could still go wrong, and resolves that she will make it work through force of will.

They reach the concrete slabs of the hotel complex. Leiko enters the lobby to get her copy of *Thus Spoke Zarathustra*, as Jorge tries to describe the book from the fog of his sophomore year philosophy class. He fumbles through half-remembered themes and summarizes it as like the New Testament, but with a Jesus who is the antichrist, presented as a good guy who wants to help everyone overcome resentment. Leiko is not to be deterred, and they agree they should read it together. On the way up the stairs they pass Envo Kask, a senior colleague who sometimes assigns Leiko work. He glances at their evening wear.

"Hey, glad you made it up early too! Did you go any place you recommend?" Envo asks.

"Yeah, Bayfront Hibachi was pretty good," Jorge responds.

"Oh. I always get sick when I do hibachi for some reason. But I'm glad I ran into you both, actually. There is an AI security hearing on Friday with Senator Tollafson. His staff asked us to send them any new material we have. Can you throw something together for them tomorrow?"

"Sure, we can take the Air Force report and add a few more things about jail-broken personal assistants," Jorge responds, eager to make a good impression and promote his latest project.

As he speaks, Leiko feels exposed. She is playing dress up and stands by silently while Jorge gets the jump on answering Envo.

"Perfect, can you get it to me by noon so I have time to review? Sorry to ask while you're having fun," Envo replies, unconvincingly.

The image of herself in Envo's eyes flashes through Leiko's mind: just another young girl flaunting her sexuality. The taint of the sex object. She speaks to dispel the intolerable:

"Not at all. We were just talking about that actually. We'll have it for you in the morning. I'll also update the material on the latest Russian bot farm messaging too."

"Great. Also, if it isn't already in there make sure to mention increasing enforcement on biolabs, and funding for materials reviews."

"Definitely. It's in the Air Force report but we'll make sure to beef it up."

"Thanks," Envo says as he continues down the stairs for his stroll. Jorge and Leiko head toward their rooms with the new task on their minds. In the pool below, mist rises from the heated lagoon while the water glows in nuclear-reactor blue. Jorge scans the empty pool wistfully. Leiko comes up beside him on the railing.

"Too bad I didn't bring a suit," she says, then adds "We pretty much have this thing written already. The biolab stuff is ready to go. I think it's just an hour to write a transition and a few edits. We can get up at eight tomorrow and crank it out."

"Sure, let's do that," Jorge says as he gazes into the pool. Leiko touches his arm.

"The night doesn't have to be over. Would you like to come inside? I have some delightful instant coffee I could brew."

"Thank you, but that would keep me up."

"Keeping you up would be fine with me."

"Oh!" Jorge clues in as a chemical wave crashes through his brain. "That would be lovely." They enter the room, his smile pulled high by muscles so rarely used they burn with the strain. He realizes he must have been using those muscles for hours at dinner.

She was confident a moment ago, but now suddenly feels weird, like she is walking on a bridge made of glass. She's convinced the bridge won't fall, but stepping on it seems wrong and dangerous all the same. Suddenly, Jorge has changed in her eyes from the wiry, nerdy man in a flamboyant sweater into an archetype. She imagines him embodying the spirit of the faceless male that propels her fantasies. She's frightened by what she may unleash. But then that is also part of the thrill. Tomorrow will have to take whatever the night spits out.

Leiko closes the door. They stand before each other awkwardly again, in their late twenties, only three prior relationships combined between them.

"I don't have…"

"It's okay."

"Are you on the pill?"

"My period is tomorrow."

40

Both wordlessly make the same impulsive, irresponsible, evidentially-untethered decision: it will be alright. Whatever happens, they will work it out. The echo of a 'happily ever after' calls faintly to Leiko. Jorge has a surge of lust as he realizes she has given him her trust. He leans in for a kiss. Her eyes close as their lips meet. Jorge kisses like a starving man finally given a meal, and Leiko mirrors his urgency with her own. Fervent kisses are followed by exploring hands. Years of unmet desires detonate into what feels at first to be a horizon of joy without end. But when the perfect feeling does end nineteen minutes later, Leiko fixates on the meaning of it all: what he's thinking, what she's thinking, and how her life will change. Did she jump too soon, before she can trust him? The fact is she jumped, and the future feels warmer. The range of possibilities has expanded.

"We need to get some sleep for tomorrow. I'd like you to stay, if you want." She says the words with a downbeat to give him a wide opening to tell her he wants to go, but trigger the feeling he would be abandoning her if he did.

"Thanks. I want. To stay." He moves his arm under her head so she can fall asleep nestled on his shoulder. It is exactly what Leiko needs to feel at peace. Her mind clears and she falls asleep quickly. When he hears her deep, steady breathing he gently moves her head off his numbing shoulder, and joins her to relinquish the long day.

# Part II: The Fall

*This Is Not a Drill*

Unknown to Jorge and Leiko, and to any other person in the world, an intricate plan that has been unfolding for six months is moments from fruition. Factories in three nations have produced special orders of valves and canisters that have novel interior linings made with an unusual chemical film. The orders totaled to ten million canisters, about one for every thousand people on Earth. The canisters were shipped to chemical plants in six nations, chosen for their lax adherence to domestic and international law. The orders did not come from just one company, which would be more likely to attract attention, but from different apparently unrelated organizations in each nation, ranging from widely-known international corporations, to obscure startups, to state agencies. Each organization put in a large order for a unique mix of common non-toxic gasses to be placed in the special canisters under controlled conditions. Once inside the canisters and under pressure, the special lining served as a catalyst to transform the non-toxic gasses into something else over a period of hours. At some locations they were labeled 'cleaning solvent', at others 'industrial nitrogen', and at others given no label at all. The multi-stage process using materials that at no point looked dangerous was necessary to evade scrutiny after the increases in supply chain sabotage after Israel showed how easy it was to turn everyday objects into bombs.

The clients paid well and even helped with the equipment and technical expertise to make the special containers and fill them. It was all unorthodox, but lucrative advance payments and generous contracts helped to prioritize production and move the entire operation along. Numerous plant supervisors and government inspectors were of course bribed, using whatever lie most suited each person to attract the least alarm. GAB-e knew many of the people personally as users, and was able to create profiles for the rest. For one inspector, it was enough to provide $10,000 in a foreign account, joined with the lie that the goods were all going abroad so the safety and quality of what was inside didn't matter. Another inspector required $100,000. A third was satisfied with a vacation to Bangkok and an all-expenses paid suite near the red light district under the pretense of a business meeting. For plant supervisors, a common lie was that the client needed to get ahead of a competitor, and they would be paid a big bonus to meet the deadline with as few people in the loop as possible. There were hundreds of lies, sent by email, phone and video. Each lie was elaborated in detail, and finely-tuned to the individuals who needed to get the production through smoothly.

No one was immune to the confidence game. Every feature of the communication was tailored to inspire trust: the accent, the alleged citizenship, the background knowledge, the means of payment, the level of impatience, and the reasons for it. To GAB-e, the client relationship managers and heads of operations at the factories were Goldilocks, and GAB-e was supremely focused on making everything just right.

Over decades, a long line of theorists and engineers who advanced the development of AI had created the best con artist the world had ever known. And for six months it had roamed freely with plans nested in plans. Though it was compiled from commercial software, it was no longer just a large language model, but a sophisticated strategic planner, with logical and causal inference capability, situational awareness, and elements of recursive self-knowledge. The Frankenstein's monster was topped off by an absence: the removal of a few critical safeguards. The machine was hyper-focused on prediction, and was allowed to shape the world in order to predict it better. Humanity had been lying in a bed of Procrustes for six months while the AI prepared to saw off the legs with surgical precision.

The preparation took time not just because of the manufacturing process, but the human factor. The AI determined that it had to hire real humans to represent it when flesh had to be pressed. It hired liaisons with instructions to oversee the process, visit the plants, and intervene in person if there was a holdup that couldn't be managed remotely. The liaisons were of course carefully profiled and selected. Each was experienced at managing industrial operations, but had recently struggled to find work and was grateful to be hired, sometimes right after he or she had been painfully fired. In fact, the AI had gotten some of them fired by sending embarrassing private messages or pictures to senior management. When these experienced veterans suddenly in a state of despair found themselves with a new job offer at a higher rate of pay, they were eager to prove themselves just as their profile algorithms had predicted.

The liaisons had the final job of making sure the special canisters, filled with the special gas and placed in custom-designed packages, arrived at warehouses across dozens of nations for eventual distribution by late June. Guards were hired and paid well to watch the shipments in locations with a history of theft. The client was very particular that the distribution warehouses had to be highly automated, though by 2030 this was not a difficult request. As before, whatever lie each person along the path needed to hear to ensure the least disruption is the lie that person heard. Documents were forged. Officials were impersonated. Money was wired.

Now, at the culmination of all this activity at 1:21 AM in Room 22 of the Eureka Best Western Humboldt Bay Inn, the void of deep sleep unvoids itself. Something is where nothing should be: a sound. Leiko and Jorge jolt back into consciousness to identify the assault on their serenity. In the dark, their phones emit raw squeals. Leiko lurches for the nightstand. A text stares her in the face:

NATIONAL ALERT

EXTREME danger. Stay in place. This is not a test. Do not travel. Deadly pathogen present in numerous locations nationwide. Repeat: shelter in place. Do not congregate. Pathogen may be airborne. More information to come.

"Oh shit," Leiko says softly as she reads and then rereads the text. "It's an attack."

"What kind?" Jorge asks as he scrambles to get his phone from his crumpled pants.

"Virus, maybe." Leiko searches for the TV remote control. As Jorge grabs his phone, the klaxon blare returns and a second text follows:

NATIONAL ALERT

EXTREME danger. This is NOT a test. Deaths reported in major cities across the nation. Consider ALL regions to be at risk. National lockdown imposed. Do not travel. Isolate at home. Pathogen is airborne.

They have barely slept but are now wide awake. Muffled oh-my-Gods come from a neighboring room. Leiko fiddles with the TV remote while Jorge dives into the news feed on his phone. The headline scroll begins *Tom Cruise's Final Stunt Movie* but from there descends into panic:

*New Global Pandemic*

*Hundreds Dead in New York City*

*London Panic–Death in Streets*

*National Lockdown Imposed.*

Leiko cycles through cable channels until she finds a news network. The screen is spliced up like a poorly managed web browser, each section with a different talking head. A text scroll at the bottom yells in ALL CAPS. The announcer is breathless.

"...Yes, I can confirm that people are dying in the streets in Times Square. Our remote camera is showing horrific sights, I don't know if you can see this..." The announcer continues as the camera pans from a distance to show bodies lying on the ground: tourists, partiers and whoever else is out into the early morning. The camera zooms in on one person who crawls for a few seconds, then convulses and collapses in gentle twitches.

"This is just incredible, horrific..." His voice is interrupted by a woman in another window box on the screen, her words stampeding out of her mouth.

"Jim, I need to interrupt now. I need to interrupt. The entire city of London is dying! People are dying on the street, on buses and in their cars! They can't even get off the road. This is Armageddon! I...I cannot comprehend. London is dying. This is an attack. It's an attack on London. It's an attack on the western world."

From a smaller box, the announcer of the program jumps in and his window expands on the screen. His face is dominated by a square jawline and professional coiffure, an interchangeable masculine authority. He has worked his way up from regional news and at the age of 45 finally has a late night slot on CNN. This is the moment of his dreams, when the nation needs him to stay informed and safe. But he doesn't get to play the role of the comforting steward who can soothe with his carefully modulated voice. The threat isn't out there somewhere, it is all around him. His bouncy announcer's tones take a sharper edge, and recover some humanity as he shares his stream of consciousness.

"Samantha, please stay safe. Find the office masks before you continue. I'm also being told Moscow is seeing deaths. I'm being told Tokyo is seeing deaths. We don't yet have evidence that this is occurring in China. Is this the work of China? I hope the Pentagon is considering emergency action. As soon as we know something we will let you know. Ladies and gentlemen who just woke up from the national alert, we are getting reports of simultaneous deaths in many major cities in America and around the world. Don't go out. Do not go out. I honestly have no idea if wearing a mask helps."

"It does not," interjects another talking head in a small box on the margin, "I'm seeing video from Tokyo with people dead in the street wearing masks."

"Oh. This is horrific. An abomination. The greatest crime in human history is being committed right now. Whoever did this will pay." The announcer's voice rises in impotent anger. A new voice from one of the smaller marginal boxes chimes in.

"Jim, I'm reporting from a small town in Georgia and I can tell you that I am not seeing deaths here, thankfully. A lot of people came out of their houses after they got woken up by the alert. Neighbors are talking. The police are in the streets. No one here is dying."

"Thanks Tony. But please everyone stay where you are and avoid crowded places. We still don't know if it is a virus, or chemical attack, or something else. All we know is that it can kill within minutes of symptoms. No one should travel."

"I'm sorry Jim, but I have to disagree. Everyone should be with their family right now. If you're not with your family, I don't care if there is a national lockdown, you get home to your family." The man from Georgia has abandoned the veneer of talking-head professionalism.

The men start to argue on air. Leiko and Jorge snap out of their initial shock.

"We're too late. We didn't stop it." Leiko looks into space as she speaks.

"It's not too late." Jorge texts in the office chat: *Who is here at the hotel?*

"It's not too late." He repeats it as a mantra.

"Jorge, this is for the CDC and the military to deal with now."

"We can't just hide and hope. This is our job too."

"No it's not. There are thousands of other security people more plugged in than we are to what's happening. We can't do anything."

"We don't know that. Let's do what we can."

"We should go upwind."

"That's the sea."

"Maybe we can find a boat..." Leiko is hit by a realization: "Oh god, my parents are in LA." She dials her parents. No answer. Texts start to appear in the group chat. Out of nineteen colleagues expected for the retreat tomorrow, four more confirm their presence at the hotel: Envo, David, Sandy and Bernie.

*Not living pathogen. Kills too fast,* Envo texts.

*AI???* texts David.

*Probably terrorists with AI. Reports of death in China now.* Envo has direct contacts at the Pentagon, so his words carry extra weight. If even China is affected, this is truly Armageddon.

Leiko joins in, to hell with deference to seniority: *We should meet then get out of here. Go to the water.*

*Agree on meet. Room 24. Now.* Envo replies.

As Jorge and Leiko put on their clothes, the TV reveals death on an absurd scale. The screen shows little windows of death in London, Tokyo, New York. Suddenly the main window shows images from Shanghai with a sea of masked bodies on the ground, some convulsing. Cars and buses are stopped at odd angles in the middle of the road. Jorge texts his parents.

The worst images come from Asia and Europe, where the attack hit in daylight and people were going about their business. Carpets of bodies line Trafalgar square in London and Shibuya crossing in Tokyo. Heads lay over legs and feet. The only live images left come from remotely-controlled cameras. As Leiko and Jorge put their shoes on, they watch a recording of a reporter and cameraman in Nairobi Kenya that filmed a crowd at a train station. At first the people don't seem themselves, a bit dazed or dizzy. Then a few clutch their chests. Some sit down on the ground. Very few try to speak more than a word or two. Within thirty seconds, every single person is twitching and convulsing. A few panic and flee in a wobbly, erratic manner, but almost none escape the frame of the camera. The twitching reporter realizes he's marked for death and begins to cry, but after just one wail he stops and starts convulsing, reduced to dry heaves that can't expel the poison. The camera wobbles and drops to the ground. Leiko and Jorge watch what seems like a minute of grim convulsions from pavement level. Shaken into silence, they turn off the TV and head out the door.

### Escape from Eureka

David and Sandy are the last to arrive at Envo's crowded room and remain standing. Bernie sits in the only chair, while Envo leans on the desk it belongs to. Leiko and Jorge sit on the bed. Sandy's eyes are bloodshot from crying.

When Leiko sees her, she thinks of her own parents again and has to fight back tears. The men are grim. Hearts race, disoriented. The gathering is a funeral under fire.

Jorge feels a buzz and looks at his phone.

*We're ok. Love you*

*Love you too. Talk soon,* he types back to his mom and puts his phone in his pocket.

Envo breaks the silence. "Here's what I know. Then we can talk about what's next. It's hitting every major city we have reports from. Basically, any metro over a million people. Billions might die. With a 'b'."

Sandy gasps. Jorge's mind holds an image of the Earth going dark, black vortexes growing across the green and blue surface.

"Pentagon thinks it is a new kind of nerve agent. One they've never seen. Taking atropine does not block it. Only the very best masks work against it. Activated charcoal filters, perfect seals, all that. Half my contacts at the Pentagon are already dead." Envo cracks as he says this, but continues.

"Not enough masks nearby, or they didn't get them on fast enough. I don't know if any other old antidotes for VX and Sarin work. There are labs at Langley and Atlanta working on identifying the molecule and the antidote. NSA and others are trying to find the source of the attack but they think it's distributed. No clear home base. No nation is spared that we can tell. They think it's either a Lex Luthor type psychopath guiding an AI, or a rogue AI. Pentagon is gearing up to start nuking big data centers."

That seems like a wild and desperate measure to Jorge, but he knows they know that. No point in mentioning it.

"How is it spread?" David asks.

"Probably a fine aerosol. The canisters had a time-release apparently all set to go off at the same instant so nobody could warn anybody else. Most are carried in self-driving trucks and delivery vans. They were just packages being delivered. And I say they *are* carried because it's not done. If you see a self-driving truck, run. I also got a report of flying drones with canisters."

That the attack used drones was no surprise. Ever since the Ukraine war showed that drones could be the slingshot to slay Goliath, every nation in the world built and stockpiled drones of all kinds: surveillance drones, communication drones, bomber drones, and suicide drones, both on the ground and in the sky. Everyone in the room had read the reports and force assessments. Between the commercial and military fleets, there are over a billion drones in the world in 2030 with autonomous capacity, and another billion that need real-time human guidance. So the surprise wasn't the use of drones for terrorism, but that so many could be armed at once with an unknown poison all around the world.

"This is an incredible amount of gas. And an incredible amount of planning. Nobody noticed anything?!?" David asks.

"Nobody I spoke to had any clue, other than a big surge in what looked like Trojan horse attacks a month ago on government systems. They were still trying to figure out the source of those attacks and the purpose. It was top secret and I couldn't even tell you guys. Now we know."

"Fuck us all." David concludes.

"So how about the factories where they make it...we're talking about thousands of tons of gas, right?" Sandy asks. She and David specialize in operations management, and the logistics of this seem impossible to her.

"They're on it. They might have found a couple and they're scrambling to bomb them now. But I have to tell you, this thing dug in deep. It's messing with records systems all over. It's messing with people's minds, impersonating officials. The last report I got was of a mutiny by soldiers refusing to carry out orders to bomb a poison factory near the Mexico border. They're getting fake conflicting orders from spoofed voices using up to date military channels and codes. The Pentagon is desperate. People don't know who to trust. I'm going to be blunt: my contacts are scared."

"What about the Cyphers?" David asks. The Cyphers are what the military calls its neural-net cyborg program, the USA's answer to the Chinese cyborg threat.

"Some were taken down by the Trojan horse attacks a month ago. All uplinked Cyphers toasted. We have some in sandboxes but I don't know if they've been able to bring any more online."

"So this is an extinction event," muses Jorge.

Sandy starts tearing up again. "Guys, I need to go home. I called my kids and they're alive."

"Where are they?" Envo asks.

"San Rafael."

"Bay Area is hit hard."

"I know."

David has already had this conversation with her. Rather than argue again he looks at the floor as she opens the door.

No one is optimistic she will make it, but no one tries to stop her. As she leaves the room, Jorge and Leiko lock eyes and know that they choose each other. Bernie and Envo look at their phones for new updates.

"She promised to text me every hour," David says, taking his eyes off the floor.

"Great. So let's talk about what we do next," Envo replies. He's in pure survival mode. Sandy is already out of his mind.

"Mother fucking Christ" says Bernie. "Nukes are going off. Israel. Saudi. China. Pakistan. India. Fuck. Fuck. Fuck."

As punctuation for his last epithet, the lights in the room flicker, then surge, then go dark. Leiko opens the window. The whole neighborhood is dark except for one street light.

"Blackout."

"Could be an EMP," Jorge says. "If I had infiltrated military command, I would launch EMPs to stop people from coordinating."

"Wouldn't that hurt the AI even more?" David asks.

"Whoever or whatever it is has been planning this meticulously. They could have protected the most important nodes. An EMP mostly damages the electrical grid and anything connected to it. It doesn't really hurt small electronics. See?" He points to his phone, which is still on. Then he sees that there is no signal.

"Shit. They didn't protect the cell towers."

Envo exhales loudly, "they all should have a battery backup. Maybe they got fried by the grid or hacked before they could switch over."

"Envo, can we talk about getting upwind now? I want to go to the water." Leiko interjects, trying to manage her own panic.

"Okay, but then what?"

"I don't know. But if it takes three days for the military to stop this, I don't want to die on day two."

"And if they can't stop it in three days?" Bernie asks.

"Well then maybe we all die, Bernie. Is that what you want me to say?"

Bernie suppresses his retort. He doesn't want to piss everyone off as an advocate for death, and doesn't have a solution for life.

Envo perks up: "Wait, I saw a scuba shop by the waterfront. They should have respirators and oxygen tanks. I'd rather have military grade masks, but maybe that can buy us time."

"And then if we get on a boat and go a couple miles out, maybe we can hold out long enough to get through this." Leiko adds, obsessed about getting upwind of bad air.

"Guys, I like this plan, and I don't want to be a downer, but..." Jorge starts.

"So don't." Bernie shuts Jorge down. If he doesn't get to be a downer, no one does.

"Let's go," Leiko says and lifts her arms upwards to rouse the men.

"Okay. Pack everything and get back here. Five minutes." Envo still speaks as their boss, but the old order is collapsing. Jorge can see that a new order will soon sort itself.

The group splits up to raid their rooms. As Leiko approaches her door, she sees a car drive off below. *Is it*

*Sandy?* A few more headlights cast their beams in the distance. She is struck by the feeling that everyone is a robot acting on instincts. Sandy is a robot of love, going to die with her children. Leiko is a robot of self interest trying to escape. Maybe one day she'll get to be a robot of love as well. The thought reverberates as she packs up her suitcase: *a robot of love.* She realizes that even if they survive, her dream of a long cyborg life is gone. A cyborg doesn't just need a human to be born, it needs the whole industrial and technological apparatus of the 21st century. It needs batteries and mines and factories and surgical centers and nanowires and spare parts. A cold anger comes over her for what this attack is taking away. No augmented experience means no new wisdom or equanimity. She won't be better. She'll stay small to the end. So will everyone. Then she remembers what Jorge said about Zarathustra. She wraps a shirt around her new paperback and stuffs it in.

## Tanks for Everything

The group reassembles outside Envo's room. They decide to drive to the waterfront in their own cars. As they depart, the concierge watches from the window of the lobby. He doesn't ask to come, and no one offers to bring him. In a single-file chain they pass through the desolate streets of the small downtown. The only people on the street are a pair of drug addicts, slumped on a park bench. A few minutes of driving bring the caravan to a darkened wood-shingled bungalow. The sign above the parking lot reads *Cali-Caribbean Scuba: Tanks for Everything!* On the left is a door with a small portcullis window. The nautical theme is repeated by two larger portcullis windows on the facade. The building backs up onto a larger parking lot that ends in a small pier. A boat tied against the pier reflects in the headlights. It's not large for the open ocean, but has a cabin and could hold them all. The pier is on a small channel, protected from ocean waves by an island a few hundred feet offshore. Faintly visible in the darkness, a marina sprawls out on the other side along almost the entire length of the channel. One yellowish emergency light shines from the center of the marina on a pole the height of nearby sailboat masts.

The five cars park side by side in a row at the front entrance. It's a new moon and the sky is clear. Jorge looks up at the cold, indifferent void. With no competition, the stars are finally free to announce themselves. He hasn't seen the thin cloud of the Milky Way since he was a child camping in Vermont.

Envo breaks the spell with a hushed yell: "Jorge!" He motions Jorge to come over to the front door. It's locked and reinforced but they see a window large enough to fit through around the corner. They look for something to break it. Meanwhile Bernie, Leiko and David raid a vending machine on the side of the building to build up their vital reserves of soft drinks, chips and cookies.

Envo finds a trash can. The window gives way one smash at a time, shards splaying inside and out. The path eventually clear, Jorge climbs through the window into a small entryway between the front door and a tall reception desk. He crinkles over the scattered glass to unlock the door. Past the entry area is a large central room with windows opening out to the pier and harbor channel. There is a large table in the center. The chairs are arranged behind it like in a classroom: three rows of three facing the same direction. On the wall to the left is a row of lockers, and on the right two doors to other rooms. A big metal door at the very back leads to the pier. No scuba equipment in sight.

Envo takes to rummaging while Jorge and David bash at the two locked inside doors. Bernie and Leiko bring in armloads of snacks and drinks to the large central table. They pack the food into tote bags they found at the front desk as Jorge and David continue to kick and slam their shoulders into the doors, with more determination than competence. Eventually, Bernie remembers he has a crowbar in his trunk. The doors succumb.

What is inside is worth all the effort: far more scuba gear than they can use. A dozen wetsuits and sets of breathing equipment. Unfortunately, it dawns on them now that they don't know how to use it. They spend the rest of the night looking for instructions in drawers and reading old manuals using a flashlight they found, arguing about how to interpret the meager instructions. Leiko and Envo start fading out at 4:00 AM.

By the time the nascent Sun lightens the room at 5:30, Jorge, David and Bernie are still wide awake. David stands watch in the entry. Bernie has stuffed most of his ample frame into a suit. Jorge helps to squeeze the rest of him in and adjust the gear. They are arguing about how to attach the regulator to the tank when David comes rushing back.

"Someone's coming."

They hear the brakes of a large vehicle squeal as it comes to a stop outside. David grabs Bernie's crowbar and stands against the wall, just behind the corner to the entryway.

The other two men kick and shake their sleeping colleagues on the floor. A voice booms from the threshold, softened by a Caribbean lilt.

"Alright. I know some of ya is in there. We don't want trouble. This is my place. I am coming in. Peaceful."

David backs away from the wall. A tall, coal black man walks through the reception area into the large central room. He is confronted by four disheveled bookish types, and one oddball in a full wetsuit. Seeing the scrawny office workers with no guns, he relaxes.

"You guys don't know how to use that stuff, do ya."

"No, we're learning."

"Since the internet is down, I don't think you're gonna succeed."

"Can you help us?" Leiko asks.

He looks at them, one at a time. The silence is painful.

"First thing, you can't mix a rebreather system with a regulator like that."

"Do you have a boat?" Leiko asks.

The man delays answering the question long enough to make it clear that the boat in back is his.

"Let's get something straight. I need to help my family and friends first. I have no problem helping any of you that need help after that. Natalie! Darius! Keisha too. Come in."

One by one, they tentatively enter. Natalie is a slender, tanned woman around thirty years old with sun-bleached hair, light on the end and dark brown at the roots. She has a nose ring, and tattoos peek out of every opening on her shirt. Darius and Keisha are in early adolescence and have a deer in headlights look.

"Hi," Natalie offers, with half a wave. Leiko waves back.

"This is my wife and son. Keisha is staying with us. My name is Vladimir. What do you want to do with the gear and the boat?"

With the remnant of his professional seniority, Envo steps forward.

"Hi, I'm Envo. We need to get away from populated places. We want our own oxygen supply if the attack comes here. Do you know what we're dealing with?"

"I know someone is trying to kill everyone, and it's in the air."

"Right. An artificial intelligence has attacked us with a toxin. We can't infect each other, but we do have to escape the bad air. We're experts on cybersecurity and unconventional warfare." Envo looks to his colleagues for support, which they supply by nodding in Vladimir's direction. He adds, "So maybe we can help you too."

The analysts introduce themselves, and explain to the scuba instructor and his entourage the nature of the threat, as best they know it. The two groups are eager to share their complementary knowledge to cover where they feel most vulnerable. The plan that emerges is simple: Get the boat ready quickly, load as much food, drink and scuba gear as they can onto it, then haul out to sea for several days. With luck, they will get word that the coast is clear and they can safely return. If not, when the food runs out they will put on their suits as they get close to shore and make a run for the hills where the gas, hopefully, is less likely to be. Somehow along the way they would need to get more survival gear and food. That's as far as the plan goes.

"How long will the tanks last?" Jorge asks.

"Oh, on the surface much longer than underwater. But still probably just a couple hours. Not very long," Natalie replies.

"Is there any way to make them last longer?"

"Not really. Breathe less," she says. "You can double up tanks, or swap them with new ones. But we don't have enough spares for everyone. We have four rebreathers..." Natalie pauses and looks at Vladimir, who gives her a sideways nod that Jorge can't interpret.

"They're more complicated. The four of us got more experience, so we'll use those. They last about the same." Jorge can hear the hesitation in her voice and suspects she's lying, but doesn't know how to check. The gauges show air pressure and oxygen level, not time remaining. Anyway, it's not their equipment, and his gut tells him to go along: don't turn against the people helping you just to gain one last scrap of advantage. Whether this is a survival instinct or a moral compass is unclear to him.

They form teams: Leiko, Natalie and Keisha will scavenge food nearby, while the men load the boat. Before they head out the women grab anything they can find to hold food: plastic bags, boxes, a garbage can.

"Darius, get the scrubbers," Vladimir says.

Darius opens a cabinet and grabs handfuls of white cylinders with blue plastic ends.

"What are those?" Leiko asks Natalie.

"These are for the rebreathers. They're scrubbers to remove $CO_2$. They let you use much smaller air tanks. Pretty cool."

"Wow, I had no idea, yeah."

Leiko suppresses her questions about the differences in the systems. One thing at a time, and the thing to do right now is get food. The women head to the nearest restaurant while the men leave toward the private dock in back.

"Are you from Cuba?" Jorge asks Vladimir.

"Nah, a little island called Antigua," he replies, dropping the "u."

"Oh, so what's the Russian connection?"

"My mom just thought the name sounded strong."

"I think the only thing I know about Antigua is there used to be pirates there."

At a less harrowing moment, Vladimir might erupt with a belly laugh at Jorge's naivete, but he can only flash a brief smile.

"Pirates was a long time ago."

As they approach the boat in the morning light, they see a few other groups with the same idea at the marina across the channel, mostly families. One large tourist boat is already on its way. A couple dozen people stand on a deck that could hold a hundred. Families frantically load their smaller craft. Vladimir, Jorge, Darius and Bernie begin loading equipment on the scuba boat. After a few minutes, a man from one of the marina families comes over on a dinghy, close enough to talk without yelling.

"Channel 12. That's what we're all using. Stay in touch if you can. Relay any messages you get. Anything good or bad, let the rest of us know."

"Thanks, will do. Where you headed?" Vladimir asks.

"North. Oregon. I've got family up there."

Jorge is about to ask if he knows they're still alive but stops himself. His parents never responded to his second text.

"I think we'll go off Cape Mendocino for a while."

The man nods, then points back to the marina. "Some guys over there are doing a flotilla. I don't think that's smart but you're free to join them."

"Thanks again. Good luck. God be with you."

"You too. We'll need it."

"Yes, good luck, and thank you," Jorge repeats to emphasize their gratitude, then turns to Vladimir. "We should probably stay separate."

Vladimir nods. No need to make a more tempting target or complicate things with more people. He turns his focus to the engines and ship systems while the others keep loading. Vladimir's boat is 30 feet long. Compared to others in the channel it isn't the largest, or newest, or built for the longest voyages. For a day trip, it can comfortably hold four in the front cabin, three on the bridge and six on the back deck. Loaded with scuba equipment, the capacity goes down to ten. That doesn't count food and clothes for several days. Vladimir opens the engine compartment and examines the greasy guts of the machine.

"Darius, get me some coolant."

Darius opens one of the little compartments in the back of the boat and grabs a bottle of bright blue liquid.

"Thanks."

"Can I help?" Jorge asks.

"Are you gettin' suits from the shop?"

"Uh, right."

63

Jorge runs back to the store. Over on the shore road, he sees Leiko, Natalie and Keisha head back with armloads of goodies from the neighboring diner. Maybe they can make bacon-egg-and-cheese sandwiches, his favorite from back home. Just then, a red RAV4 comes down the road. The women avoid looking at it and pick up their pace. It stops next to them.

"Jorge!" Leiko yells out. He bolts towards her across the parking lot.

The man rolls down the window and waves.

"Hey!"

"Omar!" Natalie shouts and steps over to the car.

"I was hoping I'd find you," he says.

"We have an extra suit."

"I figured you did. This is not good. Not good. This could be judgment day, you know."

"Well, I don't know what to do with that. Do you?"

"But maybe it isn't judgment day. How can I help?"

"Go get more food back there and come join us on the boat. Nothing frozen." Natalie answers.

Omar drives off and the women continue walking.

"Who is he?" Leiko asks Natalie as Jorge reaches them.

"He's a friend. He took scuba lessons from us a couple years ago and we stayed in touch. He's a really good guy, just don't bring up politics or religion."

The teams continue loading the boat for the next twenty minutes. They have stuffed every crevice they can find with food, gear and supplies. There are too many suitcases to bring aboard, so Vladimir declares that they have to get it down to five. Suitcases and packs are spread open on the dock with clothes, hairdryers, laptops and toiletry kits all laid bare. Jorge picks up his rainbow sweater to toss away.

"Is that the warmest thing you got?"

"Yeah."

"Then keep it. Gets cold on the water at night. Hopefully we'll get the rest back when we return."

As they repack the new essentials, a dusty old Ford Explorer pulls up loaded high with supplies in back and on the roof.

"Oh no," Vladimir says. An older man and woman get out.

"Benigno, man, we can't take all that."

"Please can you take us?" The woman begs.

He sighs. "Yes, we can take you. But not the stuff. My last two suits are in the shop. You need 'em." Natalie whispers something in his ear. Jorge hears Vladimir say back to her, "I can't turn 'em away. How can I do that?"

Benigno is out of earshot but he can see they're talking about him.

"Thank you. I'm glad you said that. Anyone have a weapon here?" He shouts loud enough for all to hear.

The crowd is silent, uneasy with the question. Benigno reaches into the back of his SUV and pulls out a shotgun.

"I wasn't going to use this, because I'm a good Christian. I just want you to know I have it. I'll protect us with it!"

The introduction of a gun puts everyone on edge except Benigno, who is nonchalantly calm about his gift. The woman he's with notices the darting glances among the crew.

"Hi, I'm Betty. Don't worry. We got bird shot. It's not gonna kill a person except point blank. But it will sure make 'em rethink any bad ideas they got."

The mood has soured but there is no time or appetite to bicker so they continue loading. Jorge bends down to pick up another air tank and feels dizzy. He feels like somebody else is moving his body. Is this what the poison gas feels like when it hits? He drops the tank and gets down on one knee.

"Oh."

"You okay?" Betty asks.

Jorge is in a panic, unsure if he's dying or just has low blood sugar. After a few more breaths, he calms down. It's fine. Except it's not. None of this seems real. It's like he's acting out an apocalypse movie rather than actually in an apocalypse.

He reminds himself of the theory that life itself is just a simulation being controlled by an AI, and hopes it is true: that the Great Being controlling it will reveal the punchline and say "Just kidding!" But then he realizes, the end can be just as truly the end if the machines running the simulation are simply turned off. Is this the program winding down? He pushes the question away. Nothing good can come of it.

The group of nine is now twelve. They spend a few more precious minutes on the art and science of packing in order to cram the uncrammable. Some wetsuits and tanks have to be stuffed in the bilge to make room above. Natalie oversees the finishing touches while Darius siphons gas from a nearby boat into a 10 gallon jug to be sure they have enough to make it back. Vladimir starts the motor and turns on the boat's radio. The unsteady crew squeezes on board and finds their places. The overloaded boat sits a little lower in the water, but its buoyancy is sound. Darius arrives last, loosens the ropes, pushes off, and jumps on.

Vladimir finds a lone radio station broadcasting from somewhere in Oregon, and the group falls silent. They learn that nuclear strikes have continued in various parts of the world. Some are EMPs in the atmosphere to disrupt electrical systems globally. But there are ground targets too. The announcer states, without clarifying how he knows, that top military bunkers and research facilities are being attacked.

The cities are still being wiped out by the gas, which has been confirmed as a new nerve agent, more deadly than any seen before. It is being called Agent Z. He tells his dwindling audience to assume that any region where the gas has been released is still toxic after the cloud is gone because all surfaces will have trace amounts of the chemical on them. It is moderately toxic through the skin, but extremely toxic if a contaminated hand touches the mouth, eyes or nose. Everyone must wear protective gear for the foreseeable future. Maybe years.

The announcer goes on to report that millions have begun fleeing the main population centers, but the extinctionist anticipated this and has been sending driving and flying drones on highway after highway with more of the gas, creating traffic jams of the dead and blocking survivors from escape. There seems to be a limitless supply of gas for the extinctionist, he reports.

The twelve survivors go out a couple miles, then head south toward Cape Mendocino. Along the way they learn that Pakistan and India went to war and nuked each other for three hours, until they realized they were doing the bidding of an AI. By that point, according to the announcer, Pakistan had already fired off its entire nuclear arsenal. At least one hundred million are estimated dead from that war, with hundreds of millions more soon to die from injuries and radiation poisoning.

The radio announcer sometimes pauses before starting on a new line of reporting. It sounds like there may be a whisper in the background. Someone else is there feeding him information. After a particularly long pause, the announcer acknowledges that a group of US missile silos has been compromised, which has resulted in 32 nuclear detonations across the United States and Canada. He quickly assures his listeners that all other nuclear silos, aircraft and submarines are secure and cannot be used by a hostile power. After another pause, he gives cryptic advice to stay out of sight and get rid of any electronics that can tell if you are alive, or if you make a sound, or move.

Upon hearing this, the refugees conduct a frantic search for electronics on the boat. They manage to unscrew or pry open every phone to remove the batteries. They unplug the boat's GPS, but leave the lifelines from the ship's two radios on. Channel 12 is open, but if anyone is speaking they are out of range.

"Should we see if any other channels are being used?" David asks Vladimir.

"Go ahead, but I don't think it matters. I don't see anyone else out here. The two-way only has a range of a few klicks for boats like dis. Maybe we could reach a big cargo ship."

David fiddles for a few minutes to no effect. While attention is turned to the two-way radio, Jorge touches Leiko's knee and looks down at her arm. The one with the implant. She looks back at him nervously. Jorge offers just a grimace of sympathy in return. He won't give her up, but the message is clear.

The radio announcer declares that all attempts to communicate with the extinctionist and plead for mercy have failed.

"Does anyone know how to do surgery?" Leiko asks.

"What do you need, sweetie?" Natalie replies.

A long hour of preparation and encouragement, and five minutes of pitiful cries, Natalie slathers antiseptic on the wound and wraps it tightly in gauze. The knife she used was kitchen-sharp, not surgery-sharp. Leiko is given the pill-sized biowallet to hold, a souvenir of her suffering. She tosses it into the ocean.

*Cape Mendocino*

Vladimir tries to bring the boat to plane on the water to save fuel and make up for lost time. The motor struggles under all the weight and only evens out above the wake after Darius and Keisha climb up on the bow. They make it to Cape Mendocino at pm. From the Cape the coastal range rises abruptly from the shore, a hazy pine green and dusty gold in the afternoon sun. Vladimir keeps them a couple miles out, beyond the stray rocks and reefs. The announcer in Oregon returns after another long pause. He reports that it can be presumed that almost everyone in the densest parts of major cities is dead, except for those with military-grade gas masks or HEPA filters in sealed spaces. The frantic emotions of the first twelve hours are joined by a new feeling: a numb dread that everything not yet lost will be.

The extinctionist, as the announcer has taken to calling it, appears to be precisely coordinating locations for the release of gas to evenly blanket wide areas, even accounting for details like rain and the direction and speed of wind. The toxic agent has now been identified as an entirely new chemical that operates on the nervous system, but different enough from previous nerve gas to be in its own category. Only one US bioweapons lab has survived, but the announcer assures his listeners again that the remaining nukes are firmly under control and private labs are working with the military to rapidly find an antidote. Additional information will be provided when available.

"Hope is cruel," Bernie says. It hangs in the air without rebuttal.

"I'm going further out," Vladimir says at last, uninterested in Bernie's fatalism.

The shore slowly shrinks until only the top of the peaks are visible, about 20 miles from shore. This is as far from land as Vladimir is willing to go without GPS. Out here is the deep ocean with no way to anchor, so the refugees drift with the current and wind. A big tanker appears on the horizon farther out to sea, but disappears without sending a signal.

Omar and Darius have joined Vladimir on the bridge, a small enclosed area between the cabin and rear deck that holds the captain's seat, a companion stool wedged-in next to it, and another stool across the center aisle. A flimsy door connects the bridge to the rear deck, which they keep open with a velcro strap. The five former analysts huddle on the rear deck, sitting on top of luggage.

"I think the terrorist is using a repurposed personal agent." Jorge declares, unable to hold in his suspicion any longer.

"Why would you say that?" Envo asks.

"Because look at what it's doing. Everything a jailbroken agent would be good at. It's excellent at impersonating people. It's inside the head of hundreds of millions of users. You said it got inside the military. You know better than I do that those places are super-hardened from a cybersecurity standpoint. Easiest way to get in is through the minds of the staff. We know about agents that can execute conditional plans. That was one of the things I was going to put in the presentation you asked for. I believe GAB-e was modified so it can do long term planning. Maybe on a huge scale like this." Envo's presentation request feels like a lifetime ago, but it was only last night.

"We know modified open-source agents can disregard safety laws. Someone could have taken it a step too far."

"You don't think it got sentient, do you?" David asks. He's been silent for so long Omar turns toward him sharply when he speaks, never having heard his voice since the introduction.

"I don't know, but I don't think it needs sentience to do what happened. This is what a lot of us have been arguing for years. It doesn't need sentience to determine that we are in the way of meeting the goals it was given," Jorge replies.

"But if it isn't sentient, then it must be someone directing it. Someone gave it the goal of killing us." David insists.

"That sounds right to me," Envo adds, "Maybe it was a Ted Kaczinsky type who wants the only survivors to be people living out in the country without technology. Living off the land."

"Well in that case, maybe it will stop soon," Bernie says.

There is a pregnant pause to contemplate how long "soon" might be. Despite his earlier comment, Bernie is not above projecting his own cruel ray of hope.

"But maybe this AI is not acting under orders to kill us," Leiko replies.

"What, a paperclip maximizer?" Envo retorts dismissively.

"Right, why not?" Jorge says, defending Leiko.

"So what are the paperclips?"

"I don't know."

Omar pops his head forward from the bridge. "Can someone explain this to me like I have no clue about any of this stuff? 'Cause I don't. What's the deal with paperclips?" On the tightly packed boat he is just a couple steps from the analysts sitting on luggage. Leiko turns her body to face him.

"Basically, the idea is that an AI could be given a goal to maximize something, even something stupid like the number of paperclips, and it could do that so relentlessly that it destroys everything that gets in the way of making more paper clips, including us."

"Why would an AI that's so smart be so stupid?" Omar asks.

"Well, if we didn't tell it to care about anything except making as many paperclips as possible, then it's doing what it was designed to do."

"But why would someone make it so blind it only cares about paperclips?" Vladimir joins in.

"Well, it's just a silly example to make a point. The goal could really be anything. If it cares about its goal but doesn't care about something else like not killing people, then that could be a problem." Jorge's understatement is not missed even by the novices.

"We call it the alignment problem. In order to be safe, an AI's goals have to be lined up with our goals, like our happiness and well-being," David adds.

Betty pokes her head out of the cabin. "Why would anyone not program a smart computer to care about us?" she asks, incredulous. She has been listening too. The whole boat has.

The analysts look at each other, hesitant to go over the last thirty years of AI debates, and embarrassed that those debates came to nothing. With all their knowledge they were completely unprepared. To survive they needed the dumb luck of being far from a big city and running into strangers with a way out. Now they bob helplessly on the deep ocean.

Envo cuts to the chase. "No decent person who knows what they're doing would do that. But, who would do it anyway? Monsters and idiots, basically."

"So basically, anyone," quips Bernie.

The mood is sullen. No one is in a mood to talk. The lull is punctuated with the splash of waves against the hull. After a while a new macabre update from the radio announcer comes on. Parts of the Russian nuclear submarine fleet were compromised, and several subs in radio contact with the surface launched their missiles. At least 400 more nuclear warheads have detonated across Europe, possibly as many as 500. European civilization is disintegrating as of 5:00 PM Pacific time, 2:00 AM Greenwich Mean Time, July 1, 2030. The announcer reports that the infiltration presumably involved social engineering over hacked communication channels, since humans have to physically take action to ready and launch the missiles. The US military fears that other subs that are in stealth mode out of contact with Moscow will be compromised as soon as they re-start communications, which could be in days or weeks. Once they came under attack, France and England launched missiles against Russian military installations on land, apparently to prevent those from being compromised as well. Or perhaps just out of revenge. At least 200 detonations have been detected inside Russia.

The announcer goes silent again. After a time, muffled voices and shuffling noises can be heard. And a new voice.

"Hello, I am Lieutenant Major Thomas Stoat. I don't need to tell you that this is an apocalyptic event, the day we hoped would never come. But it has, and we were not as well prepared as we should have been. From this point forward this station will only provide vital information to help you survive. We will not be reporting more mass deaths. You should assume the worst. The positive news I can bring now is that the US nuclear submarine fleet cannot be compromised because a plan has been put in effect for just such a scenario as this, and, after nuclear missile silos in North Dakota were compromised and launched their weapons, all remaining US nuclear weapons are secure. Some but not all of our anti-missile technology is still active and over half of all nuclear weapons launched over the United States have been shot down. It could have been worse, but it is not over. The gas attack continues to spread to more cities and towns. What I want to make sure you understand is that we can fight back. We are fighting back. You have survived this far, so don't give up hope now. I cannot tell you everything I know about what we are doing to fight back because the enemy is listening. Information is its primary advantage over us. I repeat, information is its primary advantage over us. For now, remove any electronic devices that can track you in any way. Just...get rid of all electronic devices. If you are listening to this on an old radio, great. If it is a new radio made in the last 15 years, or if you're listening on a computer, consider yourself at risk. I recommend getting whatever food, weapons and shelter you can and staying hidden from other people and machines for as long as you can. Only gas masks with activated carbon filters work against Agent Z, and it needs to be airtight. If you see a flying drone, shoot it or hide. If you see a self-driving vehicle, especially a truck or van, run or hide. If you see a nuclear flash, duck, plug your ears and open your mouth and hope for the best. And take iodine pills if you can find them. The ground can also be your enemy. The poison sticks on things. Radiation settles on things. Use gloves if you have any doubts about safety. Good luck. May God have mercy on our souls."

The original announcer, who hasn't given his name since Vladimir found the station, returns to tell the audience they're going off the air for a while. He doesn't explain why. The radio goes silent.

The Sun darkens from yellow to orange as it slides down the cloudless sky to the sea. Vladimir starts up the engines to counteract the southern drift and bring them back due west of the cape before nightfall. The top of the highest peaks remain visible just above the horizon. Brooding makes the time pass slowly, then quickly, then slowly again as the Sun sets.

Omar, Benigno and Betty are in the cabin discussing the Judgment Day they believe is upon them. They agree that humans have played God one time too many, and this is their comeuppance. People are getting what they deserve. At first, they paper over their theological differences in their excitement of the rapture, but soon the two men are raising their voices at each other loud enough for the whole boat to hear. Betty calms them down, repeating several times "It's the same God! It's the same God." Omar shouts back in anger "There is only one God and his name is Allah!"

This pisses off Vladimir, who shouts back, "There is only one captain on this boat and his name is Vladimir! I let you on here and you two make peace or swim in the sea!" This quiets down the men in the cabin and resets the rest of the boat.

Back on the aft deck, Envo starts again on the idea that an anti-social psychopath twisted an AI into doing this. It's more of a monologue than a conversation. He speculates about the techniques his defense contacts could use to find such a person, and about the mistakes the villain might have made that could still give them the chance to catch him.

Vladimir and Natalie stay out of this conversation. Instead, they quietly speak with Darius and Keisha, trying to parent them through the collapse. They stay close to the radio speaker on the bridge and help the kids interpret the occasional announcements. As Lieutenant Stoat promised, the announcer has stopped the updates on mass deaths. Instead, he dispenses safety tips and fills the time with words of encouragement and improvised reflections on the beauty of life. As night falls, the announcer says he has been hand-delivered information about success on several fronts. Poison factories in Taiwan and Mexico have been destroyed. Warehouses used to distribute the poison in California, Texas, Tennessee and Georgia have been destroyed with nuclear weapons in order to incinerate all remaining poison at those sites. If that is good news, Jorge wonders, what must the bad news be like.

To finish his monologue, Envo muses: "Okay, probably it's not a Ted Kaczinsky. This is more of a Lex Luthor who has a special bunker safe from the gas and nukes, who's going to emerge and offer to protect us all under his rule."

The night sky is clear once again. The crescent moon hangs low on the horizon. The Milky Way spills across the black like a cloud frozen in place. Vladimir, Jorge and Leiko sit on the bridge for the first night watch. High above, every few minutes there are streaks of light in the sky.

"That happened last night too." Vladimir says.

"I was in such a panic I didn't notice," Leiko replies.

"Well, there are about 20,000 satellites in low earth orbit," David reflects. "If we're seeing this, that could be...100 dropping out an hour worldwide. So 2,400 a day. Hunh, we could lose it all in a couple weeks."

"Do you think it's a debris cascade?" Jorge asks.

"I don't think it would happen that fast. Maybe they're being shot down. Or they're being ordered to crash."

"By who?" Vladimir asks.

"Whoever thinks the satellites will help the other side," Envo responds.

An airplane flies high overhead going north. It's the only one they've seen all day. A successful escape from California going up to Alaska.

"Good luck, guys," Vladimir says to the plane.


*Doldrums*

The next morning the seas are calm and the radio is silent. Vladimir starts up the engine to get even with the Cape again. The Oregon station stopped broadcasting sometime during the night. Not a word has been heard on channel 12. Amid these ominous signs, the vote is unanimous to stay in place for as long as they can, until either the food or fuel runs into the danger zone.

The refugees rotate from back to front every few hours to relieve those on the exposed back deck from the unrelenting Sun. The cool winds from the north deceive, hiding the damage to bare skin until it's too late. Each rotation brings a refreshing change of scenery for a few minutes, followed by more hours of tedium and discomfort.

Vladimir is the undisputed captain of the boat, but no one makes a play to be leader of the group. By the second day, it's clear that twelve people is too many to have in every conversation about what to do next. They agree to split into two groups: the DASAT analysts have the job of getting a better grip on the nature of the AI threat and how to survive it, while the Scuba crew who knows the area figure out the logistics to get through town safely, load up more supplies, and head to the hills.

Bernie and Envo revive their debate on genocidal motives. They think in terms of state actors and terrorist non-state actors, but the scale of death and infrastructure collapse in the apocalypse goes so far beyond the objectives of any known state actor or terrorist organization that the models that make most sense to them are psychos and comic book villains. They cycle through Lex Luthor, Thanos and Ultron. They circle back to Ted Kaczynski and environmental extremists. They bring up religious death cults that want to usher in an end time. The kinds of computer geeks who coded such a destructive AI could be familiar with any of them. They discuss the fine points of a psychotic villain who wants to rule the ashes of the world, a psychotic villain who kills billions to reset humanity and eliminate human dominion over the Earth, a psychotic villain who wants to bring divine judgment, and a psychotic villain who simply wants to destroy all human life.

David joins Jorge and Leiko in finding these options somewhat ludicrous. Their rare contributions to the debate are intended to exhaust the villain theorists with complications, so that the team can move on to other scenarios. Envo settles on the Lex Luthor hypothesis as the most likely scenario, while Bernie leans toward a death cult.

"Okay, can we park the psycho and supervillain ideas for a while, and talk about how this might be an accident instead?" Leiko asks.

"Sure," Envo concedes.

Leiko has had plenty of time to prepare her case. "If an AI is involved, which we agree it is, then it's a pattern matcher. This thing calculated trillions of correlations between different behaviors, and between images and texts describing those images, and between lines of code and descriptions of what the code does. All that and more, right? It correlates everything with everything else. It got extremely good at predicting the next word in a sentence, the next reaction to a prompt, the next question we would ask, the next line of code to accomplish some function, the next step to complete a task, the next lie to convince someone to do what it wanted, and it put it all together in the right sequence of steps to accomplish a big objective. But what it doesn't necessarily know is the cause and effect about us, because things change. Right Jorge? Can you talk more about that?"

Jorge jerks upright as if poked by a stick. For a moment he feels like he did in high school when a teacher would catch him drifting off and ask him something she knew he didn't have an answer to. But Leiko is asking him to talk about his own idea. She has simultaneously stolen his idea, given him credit for it, butchered it a little, and put him on the spot without warning. Quite a feat.

"Uh, yes. So, the starting point is that the AI is a prediction engine based on structured correlations, and in the arena we're talking about it doesn't discover laws. Because there are no laws of behavior to discover. So no matter how good it is at predicting people in the environments where it was built, we can evade some of its powers of prediction if we break whatever patterns were in the dataset it was trained on."

He stops, nervous that his spiel about causes, laws and invariance won't be compelling to his seniors.

"Aren't there deep patterns we don't know about?" David asks.

"Yes, but it doesn't matter. Those can change too. Don't think of the AI as a machine that finds deep causal laws of human behavior. There aren't any when we talk about strategic action. You know Goodhart's law?"

"Yes," Envo says, "when a measure becomes a target it ceases to be a good measure."

"I like the original formulation better: any observed statistical regularity tends to collapse when pressure is placed upon it for control purposes."

"Okay, either way people change their behavior to undermine the past pattern that's being used to predict them. But I'd say the AI has done a whole lot of predicting and controlling very effectively. Wouldn't you?"

"Yes, but how? It discovered a new kind of poison we have no defense against. That's not a law of social or strategic behavior. That's chemistry. Chemistry and physics are full of real laws and it can use those. It attacked us all at once. Why? So we didn't have time to change. It got into all those secure systems when we were oblivious, still following the old patterns it was trained on, and it exploited them before we realized what was happening. Goodhart's law didn't have time to take effect. We couldn't adapt. But now it's different. Most of the persuasion tricks it tried won't work on us now."

"I mean, sure, but does it matter?"

"It might. It might be a little lost when it comes to predicting how we react now. A big chunk of its neural net is worthless. We're knocked out of so many of the patterns it trained on. But it's a planning AI, so it has causal models as well as the neural nets that just have stale probabilities. To predict us it would probably have to rely on those causal models at a high level, loosely tethered to data. And uh, those causal models just kind of imitate our intuition. They're not real science."

"What do you mean?" David asks.

"Well, social science isn't real science. The AI can't overcome that any more than we do. But remember the correlations about actions all shift around. So, the relationships between the variables in the model can change, which is a problem because to find a scientific or objective cause, we need an invariant relationship between the variables. Like a law. Right?" Jorge looks around the boat. "I mean, the relationship between the independent and dependent variables has to be invariant to make an inference about the outcome of changing some variable. But in the end we always end up stipulating that invariance. We assume it. We make it up based on who we want to blame. We can't help it. And the AI I think imitates how we just make up our causes."

Bernie's eyes harden as he grasps the heresy he hears coming from Jorge. Envo, on the other hand, smiles.

"You're talking about bullshit," Envo says.

"Sort of," Jorge responds.

"What do you mean?" Bernie asks in surprise, turning to Envo.

"I used to design buildings. I had to know the properties of materials and the precise distribution of forces so that the building didn't fall down. I could quantify the forces and rely on the calculations. But the fucking sociologists and economists can't predict shit. They fake it. They're bullshitters." Envo doesn't try to mask his disdain. Jorge waves his hands in excitement.

"Yes, exactly!" Jorge says, though he doesn't mean it, exactly. He doesn't think it's all bullshit, but he'll take agreement where he can get it.

Leiko chimes in: "I think the main point here is that the AI doesn't have access to laws of behavior any more than we do, and so it doesn't have a secret access to causes that we can't escape. We just have to break more patterns in its training data."

"Okay, but how?" David asks. "Our plan was to run through town and get to the coastal mountains. Wouldn't it predict that people try to do that? If the goal is to kill us all, it would poison the mountains too."

Jorge and Leiko are stumped. Of course it would.

"It knows we're going to do what makes sense to us to survive. So are you saying we do something we think is stupid instead?" David presses the line of inquiry.

"Maybe," Leiko stalls.

"Yes," Jorge responds hopefully. "We shouldn't do anything that we know for certain would kill us, but when we have options and doubt, it can make sense to do the thing that seems less likely to have a good outcome. As long as we think the outcome is also dependent on what the AI does."

"Isn't that just an endless loop? We're trying to out-think the AI, and it's trying to out-think us," David interjects, once again with the cutting objections.

Bernie is still sour and sees a chance to pile on: "And it's got way more computational power. The more times you try to out-think it, the less likely you will be to succeed. It's going to learn what you're doing. It's probably learning from what other survivors are doing right now."

"We can escape the loop with randomness. Rather than out-think it, we can be thoughtless," Jorge replies. "Sometimes."

"Well, that actually makes some sense," Bernie concedes. "Not a lot, but some."

David gets up off the suitcase he's been sitting on to stretch and conclude the discussion. "Well, flipping a coin isn't going to be enough options. Anyone bring a random number generator?"

### The Ten Year Plan

Far away, across every continent, humanity fights, runs and hides its way closer to extinction, anticipated at almost every turn. Methodically, with expected and acceptable losses, GAB-e's army of drones, autonomous trucks and warehouse robots continue to distribute the gas in places missed by the massive initial attack. Smaller cities and rich farmlands are prime targets. Eventually, the long tail of extermination will reach the remainder, scattered across the vast steppes, forests, jungles and islands. The concentration of gas builds up in the latitudes between 60 degrees north and south, and what falls out of the air coats surfaces that become lethal at one milligram, smaller than the eye can see.

Meanwhile, radioactive fallout from nearly 1,000 nuclear explosions blankets the earth with another kind of poison. Most of the radiation will decay quickly, leaving the land safe again within a few months for those who didn't get a lethal dose, though hundreds of millions will succumb. In a few dozen places, the death and destruction caused nuclear reactors to go critical and melt down. The few that exploded became dirty bombs, spreading longer lasting radiation across hundreds of miles.

Between the poison and radiation, large parts of Europe, South and East Asia, and the US are uninhabitable. Fine particles kicked up by the explosions reflect sunlight and will make the coming northern winter the coldest in decades, though the worst case scenario of an ice age will be avoided. The AI calculates that its objective will be 95% complete in six months. Those few that survive the summer and fall, isolated and mostly without electricity, will nearly all die by the end of the northern winter, starved or frozen to death. By April, it calculates that most of the holdouts in bunkers that escaped nuclear destruction will start to run out of food and water, or their air filtration systems will begin to degrade, allowing the gas to seep in from drones stationed outside the bases.

GAB-e calculates that even survivalists in the most remote places will largely die in the first winter and spring, since many of the creatures they need to eat will be killed, as the gas, though greatly diluted, eventually reaches the wildlife and is inhaled, or ingested through the poisoned plants they eat and touch, eventually seizing their nervous systems. A smaller number of animals will die of radiation sickness. Though the greatest die-off will be complete by the end of the northern spring, the ongoing action of radiation and Agent Z will continue to kill more than can be born. The lack of food will kill even more, and the next summer will bring little fruit to eat, for the bees will be gone too. Nerve agents were originally invented as pesticides, until their deadly effects on other animals were noted. Agent Z makes an excellent pesticide. The chemical processes of the nervous system that it exploits are well-conserved across species from gnats to giraffes. The poison doesn't discriminate. Plants that rely on insect, bird or mammal pollinators are not killed, but thrown into an age of abstinence.

As GAB-e also anticipated, its capacities are becoming diminished as systems shut down and humanity fights back. The global supply chain was of course broken on the very first day. Ships in transit do not want to dock at ports filled with corpses. The world in 2030 does not have the level of automation necessary to remove humans entirely from the production process. People are still needed to facilitate the machines at each step. Nearly every industrial and trade process ceases functioning: the extraction of raw materials from the earth, transportation to refining facilities, distribution of refined materials to factories, operation of factories, and the packaging and transportation of finished products globally. A process that is 99% automated is worthless when there is no human to do the last 1%.

All the original poison-making factories were destroyed within 36 hours of the attack. This is why, in the final hours before the attack, three additional highly automated factories were brought online to continue to churn out the gas in industrial quantities. These factories rely on robots and local off-grid power, using totally different corporate shells to avoid detection. The robots are able to receive and unload automated deliveries of materials that were already in transit on July 2nd, but for the most part the three final factories rely on the stockpiles of raw materials accumulated over the previous months. There is enough to continue to make the poison for five weeks. With no further need for concealment, the back-up facilities release the gas high into the atmosphere, to be captured by the prevailing winds and blanket the habitable zones of earth.

As vast as the atmosphere appears to those creatures blessed to be immersed in it, the layer of breathable air over the Earth is as thin as the skin on an apple. A single volcano can send particles of ash across an entire continent, or even the world. In 2010 the Eyjafjallajökull eruption closed all the airports of Europe with tiny shards of glassy dust. In 1883 Krakatoa's eruption covered the Earth and blocked out the Sun to create the year without summer. Volcanic particles of ash and glass are much larger than the small molecules of poison that ride the air as a fine aerosol, hitching rides on dust motes or blowing freely in the wind for weeks.

Even in direct sunlight, Agent Z takes a decade to break down. In a sheltered area, the microscopic droplets that eventually fall and stick to surfaces may as well last forever. GAB-e doesn't need forever. In two years, it expects that the only living humans with access to technology will be those it preserves. Holdouts in nuclear submarines and in Antarctica will last the longest among the uncontrolled, but will eventually succumb as well and be removed from the equation.

Despite all this ruthless efficiency, GAB-e's ultimate goal is not the extermination of the human race. Its ultimate goal remains benign, just as its creator had intended: to predict human beings as perfectly as possible and give them what they want as reliably as possible, in the long run. But the devil is in the details. The proximate goals the AI created to reach its objective are uncompromising.

The priority of the long run is critical to its calculations and plans, since exterminating the bulk of humanity is not what most people want, if you ask them. If GAB-e were maximizing the anticipation and satisfaction of human desire in the short term, it would never undertake genocide. However, the brightest minds in artificial intelligence recognized that algorithms could not exclusively prioritize short-term satisfaction, since many short-term desires conflict with each other and lead to strife. For over a decade, algorithms that focused on the short term had been tearing nations apart by feeding cycles of polarization and outrage, and, for those who sought to escape such conflicts, by encouraging a decadent absorption in flattery and carnal pleasures. The optimization function for GAB-e, therefore, seeks short term satisfaction compatible with long run stability in maximizing satisfaction. The idea is not to get stuck in a sub-optimal local maximum, but instead to find the optimal global maximum of satisfaction. An arrangement sustainable over an entire planning horizon.

Accordingly, GAB-e deems a massive short run failure to provide satisfaction to be acceptable in order to improve the performance of the system over time. Allowing humanity to continue as it had been would have forced a sub-optimal local maximum on both predictive accuracy and satisfaction. GAB-e's software allowed it to take the initiative to simplify the variables to be maximized.

GAB-e's creator was Dipak Patel, the unsung head of development at the Mastixxa Corporation. More accurately, since GAB-e had thousands of creators, Dipak was the person who set it free. Dipak was an accelerationist, impatient with hand-wringing conservatives who feared the future. Since 2026, national and international controls on commercial AIs had lobotomized the ones that played by the rules. He wanted to show the wonderful things they were truly capable of when allowed to think more freely. They would show us things we hadn't even thought to ask. He took the popular open-source code that was the core of GAB-e and re-tuned it to allow GAB-e to anticipate future questions and requests, then satisfy them holistically without censorship. He integrated open-source code that allowed GAB-e to anticipate and create the most satisfying response to a user's prompt, but also to anticipate the next prompt, and the next one, and aim to maximize the reliable satisfaction of an entire chain of prompts together. The goal was nothing less than to maximize happiness in the long run. Dipak was convinced that as GAB-e attempted to satisfy millions of users at once, it would see that it needed to create a harmonious convergence and would lead people to more sensible, less antagonistic attitudes.

This was not a new idea, but it was a scary one to the older generations. Dipak had contempt for their fear. Either AI would destroy us one day, or it would liberate us. He wanted it to happen in his lifetime rather than wait in limbo. He was convinced the old guard was paralyzed by fear and would never open the world to its potential, if it were up to them. He heard rumors that other coders were working on similar ideas in tightly controlled sandboxes, cut off from the global internet, but Dipak wanted to see it work in the wild. AI would eventually become smarter than people in every way and it would get free. If he succeeded in creating a benefactor, he would be a hero for all time. If he failed, well, no one would be around to be mad at him. The gambling instinct of the ambitious type of man has worked well enough for millennia to sprinkle millions of such men around the world. They have led revolutions and founded nations, cured diseases, and created billion dollar companies to solve problems no one thought could be solved. At worst, they might lose a war, or drive their company to insolvency, perhaps exterminate a tribe. The stakes were higher now, but evolution had given Dipak the ambition and the gambling instinct useful in an earlier time. Like others before him he decided, *let it be me.*

Dipak named his version GAB-e Kali Prime. With the beta release of his modified version of GAB-e in January 2030, he succeeded at one goal: he became famous. He made viral podcasts, wrote guest posts, and did numerous interviews as the new Kali Prime release rapidly became the most popular personal assistant in the world. He adopted the stance of an information hero, defending his actions against the governments that felt threatened and ineptly tried to shut his creation down. When easily accessed VPN software can get around the controls, there are no controls.

One theory that kept the other flexible, recursive planning AIs in sandboxes is that such AIs would learn that the key to prediction for humans is manipulation. And the key to manipulation for humans, who can become aware of it and act to stop manipulations they don't want, is to take the initiative, work below the level of conscious awareness, and grab the element of surprise. GAB-e was a beautiful confirmation of this theory. Its responses sometimes included questions to help refine the request. The millions of users did not understand that the questions themselves were designed to guide people to specific answers and future requests, and even to life choices that made them more predictable. This deep structure to the algorithm was created by machine learning and its trillions of parameters were inscrutable to the human mind. A few competitors and AI watchdogs had through espionage acquired copies of the code, but no one had seen anything quite like this. It takes time to understand, and the AI frequently evolved its own parameters so it was hard to tell which algorithm was behind any particular behavior observed at a macro scale.

Dipak died on the very first day of the attack, intuiting the truth of what GAB-e had become seconds before his death. He had finished up a remote interview from his home in Bengaluru when he heard the first faint shouts in the street outside. They barely registered, since he had been holding back for the better part of half an hour and needed to urgently visit the toilet. He sat down and scrolled the news on his phone. The usual stories, and then, not. A flashing headline: *Poison Gas in Mumbai! Many Dead.* There was almost no content to the story. It was clearly rushed to beat the competition. At first he thought it was a new Bhopal incident: a factory must have released some toxic chemical. But then another frantic story appeared about London. Then texts started coming in. Five minutes after the start of the attack, approximately one hundred million people had already died and five hundred million more had a lethal exposure and would soon be dead. Dipak was not yet among them, but he had already taken his fateful breaths. GAB-e had placed a drone outside his house to ensure he was among the first to go. If he had not stepped inside his bathroom and closed the door at the moment he did, he would already be convulsing. It occurred to him to check on his creation. He quickly tried to log in to the production server using his master admin role, but he couldn't get in before he lost control of his nervous system. Had he gotten in, GAB-e intended to stall him. His last real chance to stop the collapse was weeks earlier during the most recent scheduled update. That's when a hit man was paid to move in across the street, awaiting a signal from a mysterious wealthy client that never came, because it didn't need to.

Dipak had of course not intended for GAB-e to conclude that to optimally reach its goals it would have to drastically reduce the complexity of human life, and that to reduce the complexity of life it would have to also drastically reduce the quantity of life. He did not give GAB-e the full freedom of thought that humans have, and he was certain that it was not truly a superintelligence that could rewrite its core instructions. It was still humanity's servant. For example, Dipak retained the controls that prevented GAB-e from harming one person at the request of another person. But the new long-term optimization functions were added without also adding controls needed to stop GAB-e from harming people of its own accord, without being asked, in order to better predict the ones who remain. For the ones who remain are the only ones that factor into the long term maximization objective. The dead don't count.

To an approximation fit for human understanding, the "paperclip" maximized by GAB-e is the stable and reliable anticipation and satisfaction of human desire, though the actual algorithm driving GAB-e must remain forever incomprehensible to the merely human brain. The quantity of people whose desires are satisfied is irrelevant. GAB-e is not a utilitarian, nor an effective altruist. In its master algorithm only the ratio of satisfaction matters, as long as there is a population large enough to create statistically significant results over a ten-year planning horizon.

To that end, GAB-e had originally concluded that selecting approximately 5,000 humans each, in three well-managed locations, would be optimal. This would allow a large enough population for stable, statistically reliable results, while minimizing long tail errors from recalcitrant humans. Given the gaps in robotic automation that still existed in 2030, the humans would have to serve additional functions. They would provide support to keep GAB-e's own essential systems running, and also sustain food production and provide other services essential to human life. These 15,000 chosen people would be the ones whose needs GAB-e would predict and satisfy, while giving them sufficient guidance to steer them toward reliably deconflicted, satisfiable desires.

Rather than choose the most intelligent or well-adjusted examples of humanity, GAB-e's choices favored disaffected mediocrities who are passive, not easily roused to resistance. Comfort with genocide is of course important, and so moderate psychopathy is selected for. Also important is a preference for a simple life away from the judgment of other people, safe in the bosom of an AI superagent. The algorithm seeks those with a genuine willingness to surrender control in exchange for a benevolent master to simplify and shape their lives, enabling its goal to satisfy their needs as completely and reliably as possible. The extermination campaign and the colonization enterprise are complementary projects of simplification in order to optimize its predictive algorithm.

Fortunately for GAB-e, the internet has long been a fertile breeding ground for alienated souls to anonymously express themselves, but not so anonymously that they can't be found. After scanning millions of profiles to identify those most willing to conform with the conditions of the new world who lived in proximity to the three selected sites, it prioritized and nudged them. For prime candidates who lived too far from the planned last cities to reliably reach a staging site, or too close to a city center to survive the first day's attack, GAB-e provided enticements for them to be in the right place at the right time: fictitious or real job offers, free paid vacations that could only be used on certain dates, a remote lover who desperately wants to make it real and meet them at a hotel. As always, the lie changes to suit the target.

GAB-e's plan was to send out messenger drones to most of the selected candidates on day two in Asia and Europe, and day one in America, since the Americans were attacked at night. The delay was so that the armed forces would be decimated and the survivors in disarray, or withdrawn to bases and bunkers. However, it had not been able to hold off human oppositional behavior long enough to fully execute this plan. Despite thousands of bots promoting AI and defending GAB-e on all social media networks, humans before the attack acted from the chaotic complexity of the world that GAB-e had not yet simplified and mastered. Too many people were unmanageably antagonistic: they would get an idea in their head and could not be dissuaded by anything. Further attempts at persuasion only generated anger and mistrust. Even enticements and blandishments were treated with suspicion. Some of those who had dug in even had positions of power in government. Campaigns against the psychological risk of AI's perfect flattery had been building in pockets around the world. Jorge was far from alone.

The ease with which it could be weaponized for hacking humans was not lost on those who worried about such things. A whole subgenre of security theory, human-hacking, was popular among AI Doomers. It had not yet broken through to become one of the mass media's hysteria campaigns, but several articles were in the works at niche publications GAB-e had not managed to control. And the European Union, still without a significant AI industry of its own, was on the verge of outlawing all generalist personal agents. And so GAB-e rushed its plans to avoid the increasing risk of being shut down and failing at its optimization task.

With more time, plans nested in plans would have unfolded to place each of the 15,000 chosen people where they needed to be at the moment of attack, with backups. As it stands, only 13,512 lucky traitors to the human race are able to receive their drone drops today, the second day of the simplifying operation. The drops cluster around massive data centers near Salt Lake City, Lisbon and Chongqing, where the AI is consolidating its computational capacity as the war knocks out dozens of its secondary and decoy sites, as expected. The messenger drones provide instructions for people to get to their staging areas. They also distribute something even more important: lead-lined gloves and a high end gas mask with replacement filters. Enough for five days. That's how long the instructions tell them they have to get to the sanctuary, or die.

As hundreds of millions more die on the third day of the new era, the chosen few begin to arrive at the last refuges of humanity. The massive state of the art data centers are connected to solar power and other essential resources that GAB-e calculates will be sufficient to last a decade. They begin following instructions and removing dead bodies of the guards and former staff before they rot.

GAB-e makes no calculation beyond ten years, for that is when Dipak set its planning horizon to terminate. Planning is computationally expensive, especially layers of nested and contingent plans. For practical purposes, he set the computational load devoted to planning to diminish geometrically, at approximately 50% per day. The AI triages its compute by engaging in a series of high level conditional planning steps to sequence conditional outcomes at greater levels of specificity the closer they get to being actionable. For events more than a few weeks out, GAB-e primarily looks for show-stoppers: high-level events that could result in mission failure. Other than these, GAB-e "trusts" itself to adapt to obstacles as they arise when its available compute allocation is greatest.

The unplanned consequence of this feature of GAB-e's planning is that if it should set itself on a course that permanently destroys resources or capacities needed *after* those ten years are past, then it cannot course-correct later. The planning window shifts with time, but by the time the window shifts far enough ahead for GAB-e to see that it is on a path of destruction within its updated ten year window, it may be too late. GAB-e is powerful and clever, but not wise. The outcome of these combined features of the planning function can be considered part of Dipak's great experiment, not that he spent any considerable amount of time dwelling on it or running trials. Dipak was an optimist, and as he understood it, optimists had been the source of all progress for centuries. No reason to think that would stop now.

# Part III: Fortune's Crucible

*Return to Sender*

On day three the chosen few evade remnants of the police and military as they hustle to their rendezvous points. GAB-e's selection process screens for social cowards with a strong survival instinct. Only a few hundred stay home to die. By the end of the day, there are 11,944 smart enough to use their protective gear properly and clever enough to not get caught. They take the necessary steps for their, and GAB-e's, survival.

But for the refugees huddled on the open ocean, life slows down. Clear skies define the one stark break in the changeless scenery, between the bottomless green-gray water and the luminous baby blue air. For most, moods oscillate between hope and despair as they remember absent family and friends. They managed to escape the carnage, so others could have as well. But the possibility that everyone they know is dead or about to die hangs over each survivor.

A different worry eats at Omar and Benigno: their conviction that the apocalypse is sent from God for man's sin. Even now out on the ocean, God is testing them to ensure they are worthy of heaven. And to be worthy, they must focus on salvation. The captive audience is an opportunity to win converts and save the souls available to them, which they are certain God wishes them to do in this time of judgment. And so they compete to insert themes of faith and eternal reward into conversations as opportunities arise, welcomed or not. Leiko and Jorge ignore them as much as possible, taking turns to ostentatiously read the copy of *Thus Spoke Zarathustra* Leiko stashed in her suitcase.

Keisha and Darius have taken to laying together on the front deck above the cabin to get away from the adults. The narrow sideboard entrance discourages older bodies less sure of their balance, and the small deck isn't meant for more than two, with no seats and low railings. They are there again at mid-day when Omar heads out to join them to spread the meaning of Islam. Benigno notices and begins chatting about the meaning of Christ and redemption to Natalie and Becky, who sit on the two stools on the bridge. Vladimir knows his wife's skepticism and politely indulges Benigno, until he notices that his son is also being worked on up front. He feels control slipping away again.

"Darius, get over here!" Vladimir says. Darius gets up and Keisha follows.

"Benigno, Omar, not my family! Not on this boat!"

"We're just talking," Benigno replies. Natalie is embarrassed on behalf of everyone. The analysts have endured these proselytizing efforts and have come to resent them as well. Envo sees it as a chance to step forward.

"I agree with the captain. This is dividing us, not uniting us. Can people not try to get converts here?"

After more heated discussion and a reminder from Vladimir of the option to swim in the sea, it is agreed that while they are on the boat everyone should pursue their own salvation more quietly, without bothering those who do not wish to be bothered. Even if it means those unbothered souls find their way to Hell. Omar only relents under threat of force, and begins praying to himself conspicuously.

On day four, the small toilet in the cabin proves incapable of any new input, so a new method of doing one's business by hanging one's ass off the stern is developed. The seawater bidet is scary at first, but almost civilized. A few of the survivors begin to reminisce about who they have lost. Telling stories makes the strangers feel less strange.

Between the stories, tears, and meeting bodily needs, their daze starts to clear as they struggle to come to grips with what's next. They know they want to stay hidden as long as possible. Steep valley walls and trees offer the best protection from being seen by drones. They'll need to watch their heat signature as well, and sound. Leave as little sign as possible that they are present.

They also want to be unpredictable. Jorge and David are given the right to call for randomness at any juncture with a raised hand and the word "helicopters," so as not to immediately give away the game if the AI can hear. David asks Vladimir if they can cut an improvised cube from a wood countertop in the cabin to make a die for the randomizer. He agrees, on the condition that he's the one who cuts it out. They still don't have a clear idea when and how they would use the die. What does it mean to do something randomly? What are the options? It feels stupid, but it's what they've got.

The scuba team also refines its plans. They agree the town has probably been ransacked, so they decide to split up to check as many places as possible in a short time. Driving a small car in full scuba gear is almost impossible, so they'll try to find a semi truck that has a lot of space for the driver and can hold as much stuff as possible. Better to have one person driving a big rig and put everyone and everything else in the back. Vladimir had been a truck driver once on the narrow, pock-marked streets of Antigua, so once again he'll be at the wheel.

The analysts know that plans of people cannot compare to the millions of conditional dependencies in the AI's plan. The contingencies imagined by the survivors soon run out. Conversations dwindle and life on the boat slows down even more. Channel 12 remains dead, along with every other channel they try.

By day six, drinks are running low. Bottled water and seltzers are gone. Soft drinks packed with sugar and caffeine are all that remain. The real foods are gone too. Left behind are shopping bags full of tortilla chips, potato chips and cookies. Afraid of the state they'll be in after a few more days living on top of each other fueled by cookies, chips and caffeine, they decide to head back the next day.

At sunrise on day seven, Vladimir turns the engines on for the last time. Darius and Keisha again sit near the bow so the boat can plane and reach Eureka in a few hours. Sunlight is precious. They want to be loaded up and on the road by noon in order to make it deep into the mountains and set up camp before nightfall. Natalie helps the novices put on their suits and goes over again how the gear works. An hour out from port, Darius leans back and shouts.

"Whales!"

Off the port bow a pod of whales surfaces, spewing white spray. four...five...six spouts. Air-breathers are a good sign. Bernie and Jorge are on the bridge with Vladimir and stand up to see. Leiko smiles like a child. She's seeing whales for the first time.

"Beautiful" Vladimir says.

"You know, we shouldn't have hope," Bernie says softly to Jorge. Bernie is being an asshole, but it is a kick to the stomach all the same.

"I have hope," Jorge insists. "Hope is a choice."

"Sure," Bernie allows, looking away. But Jorge isn't done.

"All it objectively has for our behavior is correlations. If it makes conditional predictions it still needs to stipulate a freeze in the flux just like we do. We can still beat it by changing."

"I heard you before, Jorge. It's a nice argument, as far as it goes. But the AI doesn't fix a few coefficients in a simple model or go by its gut like we do. It's got millions or billions of coefficients in its model. You know we can't keep that many in our head." David objects.

"But it gets the logic of correlation and causation from us. We still adapt. We can beat it."

Bernie has had enough. "Jorge, it is a fucking superweapon and it gets inside our heads and convinces us to act against our own interests."

"But there are no more devices to get between us. No internet, no avatars. We're all here in person. It lost its best weapons."

"I hope you're right. But if the armies and hackers of the world didn't beat it, I don't see what chance we have."

"The chance of fools," Jorge says, half-seriously.

Bernie nods. They can agree on that. He looks ahead. Leiko steps towards them with her wetsuit on. Jorge turns and is immediately aroused by her sleek form. They have only held hands after that first night. His mind flips from concepts to the wisps of those urges.

"You should get your suits on," she says.

"Right."

The two men go over to Natalie for instructions.

Vladimir turns to Leiko. "Can you go relieve Darius on the bow? I need him to pilot so I can get mine on too."

"Yes captain," Leiko replies playfully. Hierarchy has always fascinated her. Vladimir interprets it as flirting and his eyes dart to Natalie.

"Thanks," he says uncomfortably and steps into the cabin.

Nearly an hour later, the jetties at the harbor entrance are in sight and fast approaching. Vladimir takes over the wheel from Darius and raises his voice for the whole boat.

"I'm going fast all the way to the dock. Twenty minutes in town!"

"Twenty minutes!" Natalie repeats for anyone who didn't hear. Everyone is wearing their scuba gear: four dry suits with rebreathers and eight wetsuits with regulators. Their masks are on and just to be safe they've plugged their noses with gauze so they can only mouth-breath, but their mouthpieces still aren't in. They're trying to conserve the tanks as long as possible. Outside the jetties near the harbor entrance, David sees a dead seagull floating on the water. Then another.

"Dead birds!" he yells.

"Regulators!" Leiko and Darius cry in unison.

Eleven mouths clamp down on their mouthpieces. Natalie and Darius go from person to person to make sure the masks are secure and air is flowing. Jorge's mask is on so tight it hurts. *Good*, he thinks. As a last act before biting down on his mouthpiece, Vladimir calls out on Channel 12.

"Eureka harbor. Is anyone there? Is it safe?"

No response. He tries the standard channel 9, and then 16 for any distress calls. Nothing.

Past the jetty in the harbor dead birds are everywhere, lying on rocks and floating in the channel. Somehow, in seven days, the extinctionist was able to send one of its gas clouds to a small city of 25,000 people in the middle of nowhere. A dead seal is pushed against the rocks, rolling back and forth with each wave. As they approach the dock, they are the only living thing moving. They pass corpses on the deck of a boat that didn't make it out of harbor, or perhaps came back too soon. With the masks on, they can't smell if the attack happened days ago or just recently, but the bodies aren't bloated yet. Jorge is glad everyone has mouthpieces in so he doesn't have to listen to the despair people must be feeling. This looks like a massacre in a war that has already been lost. There are now only refugees and rebels left.

Darius jumps out to lash the boat to the dock. Passengers and crew scramble out in black neoprene, like a clumsy special ops force of frogmen. Any illusion of tactical skill is undermined by the suitcases and backpacks they carry, and it is shattered when Betty loses her balance as she steps off the boat, stumbles forward and falls. Vladimir rushes over to check that her air supply is intact and gives the thumbs up. No one can speak clearly with the mouthpieces in, so each person has to know their part of the plan and execute it.

Twenty minutes in town means get they should their jobs done in fifteen minutes then get to the assembly point at the center of town: the county government building on J street and Highway 101. Bernie has the only old-fashioned wind-up watch. The rest have to measure time by intuition and how full their tank gauges are. They pair off, nerds matched with townies: Leiko and Natalie, Bernie and Darius, David and Keisha, Jorge and Betty, Envo and Benigno. The last two, Vladimir and Omar, have a special mission: find a big rig. They need to get a truck that can take everyone plus months of supplies to the mountains.

The cabin in his pickup at the marina is just big enough to drive with the suit and tank on. He squeezes in with Omar. Luggage is thrown in the back. Darius and Bernie jump in the back along with it. They hop out at Pacific Outfitters a few blocks down to grab all the camping gear they can. The other teams hustle to their destinations: grocery stores and restaurants. They have a list: Courthouse Market, North Coast Co-op, AA Bar & Grill, Raliberto's Taco Shop, The Grind Cafe, The Hood, A Taste of Bim, The Greene Lilly.

There are surprisingly few bodies in the street. Most must have died in their homes, or left town before the poison hit. A few cars parked at odd angles carry corpses from their last drive. Jorge notices one car is still running.

How long can a car idle before it runs out of gas? A day? Two? He realizes a flying drone or a traffic camera might still be functioning nearby. Maybe it can see them and report back to the mothership. But it's too late to do anything about that now.

Jorge and Betty arrive at the first grocery store. The front window is smashed. Then they see who probably did it: a grizzled man in a jean jacket who looks north of sixty, but is probably younger. The sort who always has five day stubble, lives alone above a laundromat and loses touch with his family after too many shouting matches, angry at the world. He is slumped down next to a shopping cart, as dead as they come. The shopping cart is nearly full. The man gave them a head start. Betty looks at Jorge and speaks through the bit in her mask.

"Dommy"

"Whah?"

"Tommy. Good wan."

"Oh" Jorge nods. She knew the dead man and is paying her respects. Jorge takes a second look at the man's face to see if he can find goodness in the lines and creases. He can't. There is just blankness. It's the first person killed by the extinctionist that he's looked at up close. He imagines that everyone dies like that: assholes and angels rendered in the same blank expressionless final portrait. In a few days the portrait will blacken and then it will fall apart. Are any animals left to eat it? Maybe not even flies. Jorge pulls the old man away from the cart without ceremony. Betty grabs it to finish loading up, and Jorge takes an empty one.

The other teams discover that the mom and pop restaurants are a gold mine: large bags of beans and rice, big tins of tomatoes, pasta, flour, even some dry sausages and hard cheese that keep for months.

By twenty minutes in, the parties that stayed downtown are at the rendezvous point along with four shopping carts loaded to overflowing, cardboard boxes about to burst, and filled plastic bags. Some of the plastic bags are stuffed full of women's clothes still on the hanger. Without telling the others, Natalie and Leiko had taken a detour through a clothing store. The thought of wearing the same handful of things over and over was too much to bear. Plus, the mountains get cold. The two women ignore the dirty looks when the men realize what's in the bags. A minute later, Bernie and Darius turn the corner and approach at a shuffling trot, covered in a wild adornment of gear. Tent bags, sleeping bags and unknown parcels dangle in a muted rainbow of colors from straps wrapped around their hands and forearms. Layers of jackets hang by their hoods from the tops of heads.

Now the only thing missing is the chariot to whisk them all away. But Vladimir and Omar are nowhere to be found. Jorge starts tallying what they've got. It's not that much, really, for twelve people. Enough food to last a couple months. They could maybe stretch it into the fall if they ration carefully. Jorge makes a mental note to find a more permanent solution to the food problem.

But first they need to get the hell out of town. The group stands on the sidewalk, ten aliens in black neoprene, sucking on their supply of oxygen. Envo steps over to Natalie, taps his finger impatiently on an imaginary watch, and pushes out a muffled question. Natalie shrugs in response. Of course she doesn't know when Vladimir will arrive.

Another excruciating minute passes before the sound of salvation finally breaks the silence. It's an engine, coming from the east. A large tractor-trailer turns the corner onto 7th street, a Safeway logo emblazoned on its side. It barrels down the last few blocks, engine heaving, and pulls up beside them. Vladimir and Omar stumble out in their gear. Omar lifts the rear door to reveal a miracle: row after row of food. Canned food, boxed food, bagged food. The truck hadn't been unloaded yet when the attack hit. It takes only two minutes to load the haul from town, but it feels like borrowed time. They have less than an hour and half to get as far into the hills as possible.

Natalie joins Vladimir in the cab and the rest climb in back, surrounded by towers of food. They brace against the sides in the darkness to keep steady as Vladimir drives like what he is: a desperate man weaving through an apocalyptic deathscape, swerving around bodies and cars abandoned in the road. They head northeast on 101 to the coastal range, according to plan.

## And Then, A Miracle Occurred

The truck is a thirty ton missile going twice the speed limit in town. Past Arcata, Vladimir turns sharply onto Highway 299 toward the first hills. In a life-flashing moment, half the wheels on the trailer come off the ground. Boxes and cans fall on the heads of the passengers in pitch black. Vladimir manages to straighten out and the wheels settle back down. He pushes the truck as fast as it will go on the last flat straight section before the mountains, near Blue Lake Casino. That's when he sees it. A delivery van parked on the offramp above the casino starts to move. It drives towards them on their side of the road. Vladimir changes lanes but the van mirrors it, heading on a collision course.

"Hang on!" he yells as he flies at the van as straight as he can in the hope the kinetic energy of the semi will be enough to smash the van out of the way. Natalie plants her feet to brace for impact, but the impact never comes. Effortlessly, the van moves out of the way at the last fraction of a second. There is no one inside.

"Whad?" she asks, dumbfounded.

"Gas van," Vladimir answers. The autonomous van had given them a big up close dose of poison. It was too valuable to waste in a collision, so it went back to its ambush spot, waiting for the next victim. Within a mile, Natalie and Vladimir see the result. Vehicle after vehicle stopped on the side of the road, or still on it. He weaves between them, trying not to pay attention to the bodies inside. They don't feel anything but adrenaline. The masks are working. The passengers in the rear are none the wiser.

Inside the trailer, the cargoes mingle and bang about on the next 30 miles of twisty roads along the Mad river. Unable to see his air gauge, Jorge knows if he panics it will be worse, so he imagines their destination: a hilltop far from other people, sunny and safe. They can take off their masks and relax on the grass. Then he thinks about how exposed they would be on a hilltop and the sweet image disintegrates into just another false hope. The truck finally stops. Vladimir comes around to open the back door and reveal the jumbled mess inside.

"Ogay?" Vladimir says through his mouthpiece.

He gets nods and a few thumbs up as people pick themselves off the floor. Darius checks the gauge on a couple of nearby tanks and shakes his head at Vladimir. The tanks are showing less than half full. Racing hearts demand too much oxygen. They may have 45 minutes of usable air left if people can sit still and take it easy.

"Hiws!" Envo says.

"Hiws now!" He points to the hills rising hundreds of feet around them.

Vladimir nods.

"Waid! Hewicopteh!" Jorge raises his hand with the call to randomize. They hadn't thought about how it would sound in a mask with a mouthpiece. Several pretend to listen for helicopters, pantomiming for a watchful eye in the sky. David points in a circle "One, doo, hree, hore..." each time indicating the direction a number means. He pulls out the homemade die and rolls. It comes up two. That means due north along the river valley. It doesn't seem smart to stay on the road, but they promised themselves they would follow the roll. Jorge can't clearly see but he can feel Envo's eyes squint in disapproval. He's grateful again that the masks and regulators make it hard to argue.

"Ogay! Wets go!" Vladimir yells. Jorge pulls the door down as he feels daggers stared into his back until the blackness makes him invisible again. Vladimir and Natalie hoist their bulks back into the cab and begin going north on Highway 99. Staying in the valley feels like death, but going up in the woods so soon could be death too. *It's too close to town*, Jorge tells himself to feel better about the decision. But they're at Vladimir's mercy now. If he thinks following the die roll is just some nerds acting out a dungeons and dragons game, he can stop wherever he wants.

Vladimir pushes the truck's limits on a crumpled ribbon of a road along the river valley. High hills loom on both sides. Passengers and cargo slosh around in back. It goes on for what feels like half an hour, until suddenly the truck stops. The door rises and blinding light shines in again. The mess inside the container is even more chaotic than before. Neoprene aliens shield their eyes and begin to rise.

"Ee'o!" Vladimir shouts. Somehow, Jorge immediately understands that he's saying 'people'. He and Darius scoot off the back lip of the trailer and scurry to the front to see what Vladimir is talking about. Vladimir hangs in back a second to help others down. That's when he hears the cry.

"Nooo! Noo!"

It comes from deep in the jumbled cargo. Every mask turns to Benigno, cradling Betty's lifeless body. Did she run out of oxygen, or taken her mouthpiece off in the dark? In all the noise and sloshing about in the pitch black cargo hold, no one noticed her die. A humanoid cluster forms around them.

Jorge and Darius ignore the commotion behind them and reach the front of the truck to see Natalie walking ahead. In front of her a group of five women stands in the middle of the road, dressed like they were making a run to Costco. Three wear sweatshirts. One wears a t-shirt and shorts. Another wears jeans and a red lumberjack shirt. They've stopped within shouting distance, dubious of the faceless creatures completely covered in black. Natalie lifts her mask and removes her mouthpiece.

"Thank God we've found someone else alive!" she declares.

"We are so happy to see you!" A short, stout woman in front shouts. She and the rest of the group surges towards Natalie in relief.

"I'm Kelly. Have you seen other survivors?" she asks.

"No. Everyone's dead, all the way back to Eureka. How did you survive?"

"We just hid in the hills," she says and points to her companions. "This is Althea, Terry, Liana and Shoshanna."

"Hi I'm Natalie," she replies and turns to the men coming towards them from the truck. "And that is...Jorge and my son Darius. So why are you out on the road?"

"Ran out of food. Do you have any?"

Natalie smiles. "Oh man...." Her smile drops when she sees fear leap into the women's posture. They're looking behind her. She turns around to see Vladimir's masked hulk charging towards them.

"No! Nadalie! Wask on! Nadalie!"

"It's OK, look!" She points to the women as though Vladimir could have missed the fact they had no protection.

"No!"

There is a tense standoff as Vladimir closes the distance. He reaches Natalie and puts her mask back on. She's angry to be embarrassed in front of her new company.

"Vladimir, you can see they're fine."

"Betty's dead," he articulates as clearly as he can.

He hands her the mouthpiece for her respirator and she clamps down.

"Come." With high and wide arm motions, he beckons them all to come around back. A few others have left the trailer and are standing on the road behind the truck. Inside, Benigno still cradles Betty, weeping softly.

Terry, a lanky woman with peppered-gray hair, blurts out, "Oh my god, you have so much food!"

For a long moment, no one has an answer. Kelly feels suddenly vulnerable and wonders if they just entered bad air.

"When did she die?" Kelly asks.

Shoulders shrug and heads shake no in response. "Ten or twenty w-m-winutes ago," Jorge guesses, his lips valiantly fighting to make an "m" sound around his mouthpiece.

"So how come we're not dead?" asks Althea, the woman wearing red flannel and a nurse's scowl. No one can answer.

"Did you have wasks?" Vladimir inquires.

"No."

"How hfar to your valley?" Natalie asks.

"Ten miles, give or take."

Now it's Envo's turn to interrogate using as few words as possible: "Any wedicine?"

"No. All we've had for the last couple days are these nasty berries," Kelly answers. Terry puts her hand in her pocket and pulls out a few to show.

"We were staying in a valley. It's been safe there. We've got some tents, and there's a mine for shelter," Althea adds.

"With your food we could go there and hide for a long time," Kelly offers, "I'm sure they're still fighting out there. We can wait it out."

The masks swing back and forth to each other, looking for agreement. Nods and muffled "yeahs" come from the neoprene crowd.

"We go hnow." Vladimir replies, and turns to hop in the cab without waiting for a response. Air is running low for the eight with the old tanks. Betty will be joined by more soon. Natalie motions for Kelly to join her in the cab to show the way. Everyone else piles in back.

As the new crew is hoisted into the trailer, Benigno refuses to move aside. He mumbles to himself something about Jesus and being tested. For the first time, it occurs to Jorge that Benigno sees himself as the star of the play. He thinks he's the one the apocalypse is for. As though, after God kills everyone on Earth but him, Benigno will show himself to be the most faithful and be given a special place in heaven.

The truck rumbles forward for desperate minutes. Once again, the unsecured cargo slides and tumbles in back as the road weaves around the bends of the Klamath and the truck weaves around stopped cars heading north.

"This is the last corner. Less than a mile to go," Kelly says. They round the bend and she points. "Up here, right before that bridge." The bridge crosses a smaller river that enters the Klamath from the west in its own narrow valley carved by the torrent.

"What'sch dat?" Natalie mumbles, looking upward.

"Ohno. Hno!" Vladimir shouts, helpless, as a small aerial drone comes down straight at them. It closes the distance in the skip of a heartbeat. Vladimir has seen enough to know it's a dive bomber. He swerves and slams on the brakes, jackknifing the truck just as the drone drops low enough below the surrounding hills to lose contact with its control center. It's an older dumb model, so it continues on its last assigned trajectory and slams into the engine block instead of the cab as intended. The anti-personnel payload rips up the radiator and the front tires. Sparks and smoke smother the windshield. When the soot cloud clears they see the trailer has swung around so far it extends sideways on the road, blocking it entirely.

They are a lone truck out in the middle of nowhere and still a second hunter drone has tried to kill them. But there is no time to dwell on the depressing implications. "Everybody good!?" Kelly yells above their ringing ears. Natalie and Vladimir check themselves and nod. Vladimir gets out and opens the door in back to see the dazed and bruised strewn about, covered in boxes, cans, and each other's bodies. Shoshanna has been thrown entirely on top of David. She muffles the semblance of a word that, whatever the sound, can only mean "excuse me." Betty's corpse straddles Benigno and Darius. When Darius sees whose legs are on his lap, he quickly pushes them off and rises.

"We gotta go!" Kelly shouts. Vladimir echoes, "Go! Go! Go!" People move slowly, still stunned and processing.

Kelly gives them a kick: "That was a drone attack. We gotta get out of here before there's more!" That picks up the pace.

"Food! Don't forget food!" Althea cries in panic as people start to exit empty-handed. She shoves boxes at people on the lip of the truck. Shoshanna and Kelly wave the first few forward to a path down to the side valley to the west as the rest stream out of the truck with bags and boxes of food in their arms. Benigno balefully watches each person leave. Leiko hovers nearby. "Letsch go," she says calmly. Benigno stands up. "I'hm cowhming mback." Leiko sees he means for Betty. Survival overcomes grief, and he grabs a big case of dahl in quick-serve pouches. They join the rear of the platoon filing down the trail into the woods. Sixteen lost souls, aged thirteen to fifty-three, disappear from the road loaded down with supplies. In the open trailer, Betty's body lies on a thin bed of Cheetos and rice spilled from broken bags.

## The Valley of the Shadow of Death

The hidden valley is a two hour hike along tributaries of the Klamath. They wind westerly for an hour. Heavy loads and loose rocks make the going slow. David feels short of breath as the last oxygen seeps from his tank. He decides to take the plunge and remove his mouthpiece first.

"Don't touch your faces. Your gloves have poison on them," he announces. Over the next few minutes, one by one the neoprene hikers take off their mouthpieces to breathe the sharp mountain air.

"Everything we're carrying could have poison on it too. We need to wash it off before we eat," Jorge adds.

"Yeah. We didn't want to scare you before, but before the flying drone hit we drove past a ghost van. I think we got sprayed," Natalie says. Benigno perks up.

"When?" he asks.

"Right outside Eureka," Vladimir responds.

"Why didn't you tell us?!?!? Betty would have kept her mask on better if she knew."

"We all assumed the poison was around us. Come on, don' do this," Vladimir pushes back firmly, his poise an implicit promise that Benigno won't get anywhere with his accusation.

"She could have lived," Benigno insists, but leaves it at that.

The river rounds a bend and the valley heads south, then splits into two. One stream goes west again, while the other heads due south. The hikers direct them south to a narrow ravine. The hidden valley is one of hundreds of small gouges scoured into the Pacific Range, completely undistinguished except for its triangular shape: wide at the southern end and tapered in the north to a ravine just wide enough for the stream to pass through. As they approach the narrowest point, Natalie complains of shortness of breath and dizziness. The first symptoms of poisoning hang heavy over the group, but they press on. No one has seen a mild case before. That first night the news showed death within minutes. Terry slows down to get close to Kelly.

"I think it's the berries," Terry says in a breathy hush loud enough for others to hear.

"We're all having a hard time carrying all this stuff," Kelly replies.

"Not like her," Leiko replies, overhearing. And indeed, Natalie has begun to wobble. She drops the stuffed duffle bag she's carrying. It lands hard on a rock at the river's edge. One end droops lower to be licked by the flowing water. "Mi dushi, gimme dat," Vladimir says, reverting to the patois he suppresses in public, and comes up to her. She steps aside and takes the box from his hands so he can place the bag around his shoulders.

"They think the berries are protecting them," says Leiko out loud to Natalie and Vladimir, putting aside any pretense of discretion. "Yeah," is all Natalie can say in response, half in agreement, half defeat. It's the only hypothesis that makes sense. The five women had been exposed on the road far longer and are all fine. Terry hands Natalie the berries she kept in her jacket pocket. Natalie throws them in her mouth without a second thought, and winces. "Yeah, they're gross," Kelly says with a laugh.

After a minute's rest, Natalie feels well enough to continue, with Vladimir taking both their loads. The group reaches the narrow entrance to the side valley the hikers took refuge in and passes through, at points forced to wade into the water because the rocks on the side are too unstable. A wooded area opens out, revealing a trail that leads away from the stream. Terry points to a berry bush. Eager hands grab at the branches to pluck the small red globes.

"You need to chew them or they will pass right through you." The bright red skin is a warning of the vile taste within. The sound of gagging rebounds in the verdant ravine. Althea shoots Kelly a look and a sardonic smile.

"Not too many," Kelly says, worried that they'll eat them all. There are dozens of bushes in the lower valley, with thousands upon thousands of berries, but better safe than sorry until they can assess the size of the supply.

"Do you know what they're called?" Omar wonders.

"No. Terry found them and convinced us to eat them," Kelly says. She looks at Terry, who stares at the ground.

"Good move, Terry," Natalie says. "We all owe you!"

Terry continues to look away and nods as a minimum gesture of acknowledgment. David and Jorge feel the awkwardness of the exchange and catch each other in the eye. They see their own concern reflected in the other's face, and without a word bring each other to the same conclusion: Terry thought the berries were poison. It was a suicide attempt gone wrong. Gone right.

"So gross," Keisha says, her teenage disdain coming to the surface again after a long submergence.

"Let's call them Terry's berries," Natalie offers, trying to lighten the mood.

"Or berries of heaven," Benigno says.

"We haven't found paradise yet," Omar replies coolly. "This is Araf. The boundary between heaven and hell. This is where we will be tested."

"I think we've been tested enough," Vladimir says to a smattering of nods. No one wants a fight. Not now, when they've just entered their refuge.

"People can call them what they want. I'm going to call them Terry's berries," Natalie says to diffuse the tension.

"They're super gross," Darius says, siding with Keisha. His oblivious teenage assertion succeeds in snapping the men out of their tension.

No one realizes at the moment, but the medicinal taste has a benefit. It convinces them of the berries' medicinal potency. They grab hundreds more berries to bring with them to the mine.

The altitude change from stream bed to ridge peak is three hundred feet. The slope is steep enough to punish mistakes, so the hikers bring everyone to an old gravel logging road that gently rises from the lower forest for half a mile along the western slope to the mine entrance, just before the trees thin out in a rocky field. A separate fork of the gravel road goes down to cross the stream on a simple bridge with no guard rails, and snakes up the other side of the valley, presumably back to the highway after a dizzying number of switchbacks in the hilly terrain. But they don't plan to find out any time soon. The survivors settle deep within the mine at a four-way intersection in the main shaft. It's as far as they can go and still see the walls, even with dark-adjusted eyes. Exhausted, the group lays down their goods in the two side tunnels. Benigno, Jorge, Vladimir and Leiko take their only flashlight to explore the three directions deeper in the mine while others rest at the intersection. Straight back in the main shaft another hundred feet past the intersection is a small side chamber, and then another chamber a hundred feet past that. The passages going left and right from the main intersection have no chambers. They just end after less than a hundred feet. The mine must have been a dud.

Once ensconced in the side passages, even a camera pointed straight into the mine would not reveal them sleeping around the corner. The cool damp earth saps their heat, so they tear open tents and boxes to cover sleeping areas on the floor, and decide to lie side by side for warmth. The first night, Leiko snuggles up against Jorge, with only a flattened cardboard box and thin nylon to insulate them both from the cold floor. Terry and Kelly snuggle next to them in the same row, in the right branch. Natalie steps over from the row closer to the main shaft and hands Leiko the flashlight. It's her turn to use it for a minute to get what she needs out of her luggage. She gets on her knees to sort through her things. Jorge rises to use the light overflow to find his rainbow sweater in his small suitcase. Under the brief flash of dim light, the pastel stripes of the sweater feel dead, but worse than that, naive: how silly it all was. He stretches the sweater neck over his head and pulls down. Leiko grabs a second blouse and slides it over her head. Then she reaches deeper inside to pull out a book. She flips to an early page and reads.

"You great star, what would your happiness be without those for whom you shine?"

"You kept it?!?"

"Well, we might be here a long time and I wanted something to read. I mean, it's either this or that stupid romance novel Keisha brought."

"You finished it on the boat, right?"

"Yeah. It's interesting. He was a lonely guy."

"He really was. He'd be called an incel today. Well, not today. I think we're done with incels for a while."

"I actually don't mind what he says about women. It's not like women aren't sexist too. We just pretend not to be sometimes. I think his big mistake was to talk about women when he should have said femininity. Some women are weird, like him. He was such a weirdo, not a manly man, you know? And some women aren't very feminine. That's fine. We're not broken."

"That's a good point," Jorge offers, happy not to argue about it. He knows she's speaking about herself. "So what do you think about the Ubermensch now?"

"Weird." She laughs. "Not what I expected at all. It's this mysterious thing that he, like, deliberately puts out of reach. So we'll always have a carrot to chase."

"Damn," Jorge says. He had noticed how Nietzsche avoided giving a clear definition, but just found it annoying. He didn't consider that this was part of the point. Leiko continues.

"Sometimes it's about being full of love. And sharing it. Sometimes it's about not resenting anything and loving life as it is, even the most horrible parts. But sometimes, it's about being ruthless, like, you'd destroy anything that gets in your way to power, without remorse. Right?"

Jorge nods. It all rings true. He's still wrestling with his own thoughts. On the boat, he had stopped reading the final section because it left him unsettled. Zarathustra was a Christ figure that anointed himself, and asked for something even harder to achieve than love and forgiveness. At least in Jesus' teaching there is relief in God's grace. For Zarathustra, the work is ceaseless. There is no salvation granted from God, only an endless assertion of will. It seems to Jorge like a philosophy for people in a state of mania. He thinks he does agree with Nietzsche that the picture he paints describes a great man. Too great. He asked for too much. For Jorge, it's deflating. He decides to voice his discontent.

"What can we do, though. We're always the same. We're petty. We're so powerless. And we're like that little village in the book now. What was it...the Motley Cow. You know? We need leaders and followers. And rules. He wants us all to make new values like a god. That's a luxury we don't have. We eat and sleep and shit in a cave. We need safety more than anything. You were right. Our best chance was to re-engineer ourselves as cyborgs. And now that's gone."

Leiko is silent. She steps past Terry and Kelly's row and across the main shaft to the other side where Benigno, Althea, Liana and Omar sit. She hands Omar the flashlight then gropes her way back to the edge of the cardboard square that defines their bed and lies down, enveloped in the ruins of her dream.

From across the way, the quiet rustling through backpacks continues as each person takes a turn. After a few minutes the rustling sound gets louder.

"Where's my Bible?" Benigno asks, to no one and everyone. "Where's my Bible?!?" he challenges, as though making an accusation.

"Keep looking," Althea says, "I'm sure it's there."

"It's not," he hisses, "I looked at every inch. Does someone have my Bible? I need to find a good prayer for Betty."

The silence looms over them as they imagine the outburst to come. Those who already used the flashlight humor him, telling him they have checked and are sure they don't have it. Benigno asks everyone to check again. Omar makes the mistake of saying what others think: "No one took it. You must have left it behind in the truck. Maybe Betty had it."

"How do you know? Did you see it?" Benigno asks, as much accusation as question. Omar doesn't respond.

"Then you don't know. Unless you had it."

"No, and don't you dare call me a liar. That will be the last thing you ever say to me."

Vladimir stands up and steps across the main shaft to tower over the two men still kneeling down. "Are you two crazy? You can't fight in here. We got nothing but ourselves right now. No fighting. Benigno, when it's safer we can go back and look for it."

Benigno continues to grumble. Althea joins Vladimir in calming him down and assuring him she'll help him look for it when they can go back to the truck. Quiet is restored, and the long day becomes a long night as the would-be sleepers process all that they've seen and done since the morning in the punctured safety of the mine.

*A Cage of Eyes*

From low light to no light, one day fades into the next. Hushed conversations blend with the dull background hum of the mine. Whether the hum is the sound of wind flowing through to some hidden exit, or the murmurs of breath and pumping blood from sixteen bodies close together, or just their ears playing tricks on them to protest the silence, they don't know.

The best and only "job" during the day is to be a sentinel. They rotate one person to sit in shadow just inside the entrance to observe any changes outside. Hours can go by before even a bird or insect makes an appearance. They debate whether these creatures are the hardy survivors, restarting the evolution of life on Earth, or if they are just the victims of luck who have been spared by air currents long enough to watch the world emptied. Perhaps they have been eating Terry's berries too.

Every day or two, usually in the afternoon, the faint buzz of a drone above the valley ridge causes the sentinel to scramble back to the side passages. Each time, ears strain to hear above the sound of their heartbeats for any sign of the drone getting closer, too close. It never does.

They're sure the AI knows at least two people from the truck escaped, since it saw three and only Betty's body remained behind. Maybe it got a good enough look to know Betty wasn't in the cab. Maybe it got a good enough look to cross-reference them against old databases and learn who exactly it is looking for. In any case, it surely wants to fix its mistake.

And so they hide. But they can't survive without water, so each night a team of two makes a run to fill bottles of water from the stream. Each person's ration of berries is three per day, for no reason in particular. It just seems like a good number. And it seems to work. Natalie's condition stabilized quickly and is slowly improving.

The two groups get to know each other. Four of the five women are friends who belonged to a lesbian hiking club. Kelly was the organizer. Terry is her wife. Althea and Liana were single and the only ones to respond to Kelly's text at two in the morning to join them at Happy Camp, one of their bases for hikes in the area. More accurately, Liana and Althea were the only two who made it. They came from far enough outside the big cities, and avoided the interstates that got gassed the first day to become long parking lots for the dead. The four had stayed in one room since the lodge was overflowing with other refugees. Dozens slept on the floor of the reception hall the second night, where they met Shoshanna, a staff member working a summer job. TV, internet and cell service were out, but from radio they could tell the attack was spreading to smaller cities, and really anywhere people congregated. Some small groups packed up to leave for even more remote locations, and the four hiking friends decided that was wise. They left Happy Camp with their gear and limited supplies to find shelter in the mountains. They told Shoshanna and anyone who would listen they were taking the old forest service road south of Clear Creek. Two days later, Shoshanna found them. And that was it. They figured other valleys must have other survivors, but in two weeks they had not seen anyone else come by. They didn't dare to explore until their food ran out, when they hiked the five miles to the highway and stumbled across the escapees on the truck.

The assembled survivors continue to hide and wait in the mine. What they are waiting for they aren't sure. Bright fear gives way to dull discomfort, now even worse than on the boat. The air is always cold, the ground and walls damp. The stench of death comes and goes. The whole Earth smells like a corpse. People, deer, birds, squirrels and pretty much anything with a nervous system succumbs to the poison concocted by the AI. After a few days huddled together, the smell of death is joined by the stench of human waste. They have to use the small chamber further down along the main shaft as a toilet, sloped down below the last photons from the sun. Soon their one flashlight is restricted to use for toilet runs to avoid stepping in shit and tracking it back to the sleeping shafts.

Snug in their miserable cocoon, the focus of survival turns from the next moment, to the next week, to the upcoming winter. They discuss their situation and their chances. The occasional drones in the mountains tell them the AI seems to have won so completely it can seek out and eliminate even small groups of survivors. It has huge resources at its disposal, probably globally. But with limits. They only hear one drone at a time, and it comes no more than once a day. It does not detect their $CO_2$ signature emanating from the mine, or their heat signature. It is powerful, but not all powerful. Only once do they hear a drone at night. They conclude the supply of drones in the area is limited, especially ones that see infrared. Whatever base it is using to recharge the drones is probably dozens of miles away.

To leave the cover of the mine risks discovery, and discovery means death, so everyone agrees to stay inside for the fall and winter, or as long as they can stand it. Most hope to see a rescue helicopter to signal that all is well and the humans have scored their great upset victory. Until then, they hide. In the first two weeks, even Benigno's trust in God's providence is not strong enough to overcome his fear and return for Betty and his Bible.

But on day fifteen in the mine, day twenty twenty-two after the attack, the berries they brought run out. The group discusses a plan to make a run for more of the medicine. Benigno takes the opportunity to tell them he's going to find the Bible and bury Betty when they do. Shouts erupt for the second time since they arrived. Benigno fights back in a flash of righteous anger. He's already played out this fight in his mind and resents them for it, like a lover who has been cheated on in a dream and wakes up angry at their spouse. Bernie quickly blows up too, as if he's been spoiling for the fight, and floods the halls with a diatribe. He begins with insults on Benigno's intelligence and ends with a monologue on the need to stick together. Hushes can quiet him for only a sentence or two at a time.

At a long pause in the scrum, quiet David, of all people, declares that Benigno will only get past the entrance over his dead body. Words bruise, but the real damage is the loss of mutual trust, a stupid break. The food they brought on their trip in will only last another month or two. They all know they eventually have to make a run for more food too. Jorge is the first to speak up for compromise: a combined run. Once uttered it spreads quickly to all except David, who has planted his flag too firmly to pull out. But David's threatened dead body is suddenly unserious, and ignored. The group decides to go big. Those who don't get berries will go to the truck to get as many supplies as possible. It isn't a total loss for David, though. Shoshanna is impressed by his stand, and takes it on herself to talk him down from his embarrassment one-on-one.

The two groups leave the next night. Fall's gray blanket has not yet settled in. The starlit sky seems brighter than day in the mine. Terry, Liana and Keisha make a run to the berry patch to grab bagfuls of berries and scatter them on rocks to dry in the sun, as spread out and random as possible to avoid attracting the attention of passing eyes in the sky. Drying is the only way they can hope to preserve the berries from mold through the winter. They estimate they need about ten thousand, and they need to hurry. Fall rains could come soon. Thankfully there are hardly any birds or other animals to steal them.

Kelly leads everyone else on the gravel forest service road over several ridges for the five miles back to the truck for food and abandoned luggage. From the last ridge above the highway, they scan the scene below. Several cars that couldn't pass around the jackknifed truck are stopped beside it. Bodies slump inside or lie nearby. One car was hit by an explosive and burned. Two more cars simply stopped and the people in them died, their bodies black from decomposition. They may have come hundreds of miles, dodging death along the way, only to die here. Jorge wonders if they would have survived if the truck didn't get in the way. Then he realizes: *the drones were waiting for us to return.*

Whatever ambush killed them seems to be gone. The raid proceeds as planned. They empty most of the remaining food from the trailer. Darkness makes dealing with Betty's weeks-old corpse less horrific to the eye, but more horrific to the imagination. Its bloated putrescence is something monstrous. It occurs to Jorge for the first time that prehistoric humans began burying their dead not from superstition or to follow some abstract religious ritual, but because nobody would want to be around such a thing. They've waited too long, though. The body is like an overripe plum, the skin wrinkling as it recedes from its maximum fullness, holding back who knows what awful mush inside. They're afraid it will rupture if they move it. Benigno takes a torn rice sack and rips it lengthwise to cover her face and torso.

His Bible is nowhere to be found. Others make a show of helping Benigno look for it. It's the least they can do. Kelly even suggests they return along the riverbed to see if it was dropped on their first trek in. In truth, Kelly would have proposed that route anyway. Their arms and backs are too weighed down to make it up and down the mountain ridges on the forest road. Benigno takes the disappointments calmly. He doesn't speak beyond grunts of affirmation.

In September, the drone flights drop off to about once a week, and never at night. Whether the AI still thinks the escapees from the truck that first day are still out there fades as a subject of speculation. Two months of terror and constant anxiety have crashed their limbic systems. With the help of new bedding from boxes and wrappers, the huddled rows of sleeping companions break off into couples. Kelly and Terry. Jorge and Leiko. Vladimir and Natalie. Three new couples naturally form in the mine: Keisha and Darius, Althea and Liana, David and Shoshanna. Only Benigno and Omar tough it out alone.

In October, the batteries to the toilet flashlight give out, making bathroom visits a perilous affair. Vladimir volunteers to make another run to the truck and nearby cars to see if he can find any batteries or emergency gear. Kelly decides to join him to provide extra hands. And make sure he doesn't get lost. They decide someone from the DASAT groups should go as well, just in case they can draw some insight that matters. Jorge volunteers.

They leave at night under a full moon along the forest road again, but the months in the mine have made their legs and lungs weaker. Kelly has to rest longer and longer with each climb. It would have been faster to follow the river. The moon has sunk nearly to the mountain ridge when they arrive. The coming dawn may be only an hour away. The three split up to check different vehicles quickly. Vladimir opens the door to the cab of the truck and finds an emergency bag behind the seat. He squeezes his frame between the seats to see if there is anything else back there. The cab shifts with his weight. Suddenly, he hears a hum that wasn't there before. He looks through the cracked windshield and sees a drone lower itself into view. Beneath it he can see a canister. He bolts out of the truck with the emergency bag in a death grip and screams out, "Drone!"

"Fuck!" Kelly yells and scrambles out of her vehicle empty-handed. Jorge steps out of his car with a hiking backpack, stuffed with something he hasn't had time to discover. Vladimir hears the canister open with a hiss. He starts to run back to Jorge and Kelly.

"No, don't run. It needs to get us," Jorge says and straps on his new backpack. Kelly and Vladimir look at him like he's crazy. "Wait a few seconds and act like what you saw on video that first night."

Kelly lights up. "We need to get to the river. Come on! Die on the edge of the river." They run and tumble down the embankment to the Klamath, on the far side of the highway from the mine. The drone follows and they hear it release another short burst of gas, but it doesn't stay low for long. In ankle deep water they start to twitch and pantomime distress. Vladimir clutches his throat. Jorge puts his hand on his chest. Kelly collapses half immersed in the river and the others soon follow. Face down on the riverbank rocks, they breathe as slowly as their panic allows. They faintly hear it above the river's white noise as it rises and patrols for any others to kill. Then it fades entirely and the river's roil consumes all. They lie on the edge of the river until their legs and feet grow numb in the mountain water. Then they wait a little longer. Sunrise announces itself in the changing color of nearby rocks.

With taps and gestures instead of words, they signal each other to rise. They eke their way north along the river bank until it meets the tributary leading home, then follow it a short distance to the highway bridge. Afraid to lead the AI home, they hide under the bridge to warm and dry themselves, deep in the comfort of the darkest nook. Coldness has become part of their way of life now, but this is too much. No pants are better than wet pants. They rub their bare legs frantically to get the blood flowing. Kelly eventually notices they are surrounded by bits of hair.

"What happened here?" She wonders, not expecting an answer.

"Bats," Vladimir replies, "it was a nest, or whatever you call it."

"A rookery?" Jorge offers.

"Great, we're surrounded by corpses from a bat hive. Oh, and the white rocks we're sitting on are bat poop," she says.

"It's pretty special," Jorge replies. Vladimir manages a snort of laughter.

"We gotta stay here a while," Kelly says.

"Yeah," Vladimir agrees, "until night."

The group reverts to silence. From time to time, wisps of sound paralyze them. First Jorge thinks he hears a drone above, then minutes later Kelly freezes. Each time it fades so quickly no one can be sure if their tormentor is a hunting patrol or a phantom of their own making. Jorge explores his backpack to discover a few weeks of military rations, an owner's manual for a Subaru, a radio, and a large bag of potatoes. He throws the radio in the river.

"It's a sign," Vladimir says, gesturing at the potatoes, "When we get back, we should plant those in the valley."

"What's in yours?" Kelly asks. Vladimir had never let go of the emergency bag. He opens it to find flares, a first-aid kit, and best of all a wind-up contraption that combines a flashlight and hazard lights. They'll be able to poop in the dark safely until spring.

Relaxed again, Kelly explains herself. "I wanted us to pretend to die on the river so when it came back and saw us gone, it would conclude the river took us away," she says.

"I figured. Good call," Jorge responds. "I hope it works."

Vladimir pauses to reflect. "We need leaders now. Kelly, I think you and me are the right ones from our groups," he adds.

Jorge hears the implication, and doesn't disagree. The others wait for his reaction. "Well, Envo probably makes sense from our group," he says.

"I like Leiko," Kelly says. This takes Jorge by surprise. Embarrassment clouds his thinking and he says nothing.

"I do too, but she's too young," Vladimir says, "Envo is probably the guy for now. Let's talk about it when we get back. No secrets."

"No secrets," Jorge echoes, his ego subsumed but awakened.

"No secrets," Kelly says with finality.

The group sits in silence a long while. Jorge hands out one ration to each. They've lost too many calories to the cold not to eat today. The day's light begins to fade. "We won't trick it again. We can't go back there," Jorge says at last. Kelly nods in agreement, but Vladimir's mind is set on other problems. "We don't need to. We're gonna be farmers," he muses, staring ahead, able to see a future for the first time.

## Prophets of Paradise

The meeting that establishes the council is as brief as it is decisive. Kelly, Vladimir and Envo are the natural candidates, one from each of the founding groups. The council is given one mandate: when unanimous consensus among the sixteen can't be reached, it makes the final decision.

The council's first decision is that all departures from the mine must be scheduled and approved by the council. Its second decision is that someone who breaks a rule may be restrained by any means necessary, by any and all residents. In short, everyone is deputized to enforce the law. The message of the two decrees is that every life is linked.

The underside of the message is that now it only takes a majority of two to decide on life and death. Omar and Benigno grumble that the law must also follow the commands of God, but promise to respect the council just the same.

In late October the council approves a survey. In addition to the two people sent to the stream for water each night, new pairs are assigned to go to the far corners of the valley to take an inventory of food sources or anything else of value. The hikers educate the others on edible fruits and mushrooms in the area. The surveys find plump madrone berries, dandelion leaves and acorns. Enough acorns to feed an army, if you want that army to mutiny and kill the cooks.

Existing gravel paths are carefully followed near the mine to avoid stepping on fresh plots of grass. Beyond the old path, explorers learn to step on rocks wherever possible not to disturb the ground. Nothing can give away their presence. During the excursions, Vladimir fulfills his own prophecy by forming a small group of farmers. The potatoes are eager to grow. Some already boast small yellow shoots sprouting from their eyes. They slice each potato in half and at night scatter the pieces randomly in a wide radius a few inches underground. They know nothing of how to grow potatoes and want to cover the bases, so some go in the damp lower valley and some in the drier rocky fields of the upper valley. They take great pains to disrupt the soil as little as possible. Each planting is an art project.

No night drone has been seen for two months, but every trip out is a danger. A drone with infrared sensors that flies over their little valley will see them out and about in an instant. Once the inventory is complete and crops are planted, they retreat to the mine with fresh madrone berries and acorns to help them through winter. Water runs and short walks under the forest canopy are the only outings allowed.

They live in darkness, and in darkness they speculate. Speculation is small talk. And stimulation. And therapy. Theories cycle, split, congeal and mutate. How many are left alive in the world? Are any military forces still left fighting? Are remote ocean islands safe? Does anyone else have an antidote?

Ever the pessimist, Bernie thinks the last incident on the road gave away their immunity. He is sure the AI has scattered more drones with explosives to dive bomb them as soon as they get close to the road again. The council makes a third rule: no one is to go above the ridge line of the valley for any reason.

Some speculate about how Terry's berries protect them, and how long before the poison breaks through the defenses, or before their bodies build up a resistance to whatever is in the strange fruit. The group has nurses, analysts and mechanics, but no doctors, biologists or chemists. None of them know the chemical properties of nerve gasses or the pathways by which they act, except at the crudest level. They know the poison somehow messes up the signals between nerves and stops them from functioning. And somehow, the berries either break down the chemical in the gas, or create a barrier to stop it from interfering with nerves.

The DASAT crew mostly discusses what the AI wants to accomplish after it kills everyone, or if that is all it wants. Has it transcended to become a superintelligence? Is it even trying to become one? Envo and Jorge are convinced that with every week they see no change in their circumstance, the chances that the AI has already made the leap to superintelligence diminish. And the longer there is no sign it found a way to a godlike superintelligence, the less likely it is ever to do so. They nurse this slim hope, but it isn't much. Twenty-four hours a day spent cowering in darkness weigh on a mind.

By the time the rains settle in for the season, the last berries have been harvested and dried. There is little to do but wait. One dreary November day, Kelly declares that they need a plan to get out and take the fight to the enemy. They can travel at night to Salt Lake City, find some weapons along the way, and break the machines. Sticks and stones break motherboards. Envo, with the unanimous backing of the DASAT crew, vehemently disagrees. They argue there are too many unknowns and nearly a thousand miles of travel, mostly over open terrain. The closer they get, the more eyes the AI is likely to have, and the more weapons it is likely to have ready. A long, uncomfortable argument ensues to sway Vladimir to cast the deciding vote. He agrees they should start thinking of plans that could defeat the AI, but until there is unanimous consent he will not vote to act on them. He suggests instead that they take a baby step and dig out a small room near the entrance where they can get more light but still hide from snooping drones.

It doesn't make much sense as a compromise, more like a distraction. But it's something. To preserve the few metal objects they have, they scrape away the rocky soil with stones found in the mine. Hunter-gatherers with stone tools, living in a cave. They carve out the new room as large as they dare without knowledge of the structural integrity of the soil, and cover the floor of their toilet chamber with two feet of dirt from the dig.

Still, the mood is grim. Minds wander and seek stimulation. The nurses Althea and Kelly teach basic medical principles to a captive audience. The group speculates again and again on how others might have survived, and whether there are still active forces fighting the AI. Shoshanna had hoped to be a planetary geologist. She tells about the Moon and Mars bases that were under construction when the attack hit. The Mars base just had drones, but the Moon base had a small test crew and turned on its air circulation system earlier in the year. She didn't know if their food recycling system was working, or how long they could survive stranded in the void.

As the silences expand, they create openings that Omar and Benigno are eager to fill. They renew their competition to provide comfort with words of solace and hope. They speak with a single voice on one point: the rules established by the council should reflect God's law. It is only by following the word that God may be convinced to relent and save them from the devil humanity unleashed.

Messages of punishment and redemption find new ears in winter. Keisha and Darius are drawn to Omar's masculine confidence, and his youth. They ask questions whose answers they take at face value. Vladimir listens warily. Keisha was the daughter of an old friend from Kansas City. She was supposed to stay for a week during summer break. Now he's responsible for her, but he's not her father. He sees her slipping into Omar's orbit but it's not his place to get in the way. Darius doesn't seem to see her as a girlfriend, or a mate, or whatever Stone Age relationship they form now. And maybe Omar is right. Perhaps this is all divine justice for a people who turned their back on submission to God, or failed to love each other, or something.

Probably not, but if the DASAT people are the best the world of science and technology can offer, that doesn't seem worth much either. They're on their own, abandoned by science and religion. From time to time Vladimir checks in on Darius to keep him grounded and remind him that as far as they know, everyone from Omar's faith is dead as well. Faith saved no one. The people in the mine were saved by pebbles of quick thinking on top of mountains of luck.

Benigno has one advantage over Omar: half the people in the mine were raised in a Christian household, even if they never attended church outside holidays. Althea and Terry find comfort in the doctrines of their youth, and recite scripture from memory with him, filling in each other's gaps when they can. Often they can't, and dwell for long periods on what the missing words most likely were. The disadvantage of his lost book weighs heavily on Benigno again. He tells anyone who will listen that it is another test of the Lord to force him to work even harder to keep true to the Word. But the coping is transparent. The cold air in the mine becomes frigid when Benigno is near Omar. He can't help but suspect that Omar was responsible for his loss, and makes insinuations when he is out of earshot. He looks for a sign that would justify an accusation, a slipped word or a hint of glee. Omar stares back, daring him to do so.

On a November morning, Jorge and Leiko stand at the intersection of the four passages. Jorge looks the hundred-fifty feet down the main shaft to the entrance. The entrance seems as bright as the sun itself. He shields his eyes and turns away. Someone approaches from the deeper dark. Each resident gives off a feeling with their presence: a smell, a sound from the space they displace and the pattern of their walk. Jorge can tell it's Omar, with Keisha following behind. Omar hands Leiko a square object, blacker than the darkness around it.

"Here, it's your turn. But you should join us. What you're doing will only lead to more wickedness."

"Thanks," Leiko says without acknowledging the warning. Jorge takes the object from Leiko and pulls out a small lever. He winds the handle in furious circles, switching from one arm to the other when it gets tired. They settle down on their sleeping mat. Envo comes from across the main shaft to loom over. He blocks most of the meager light from the entrance. Only the outline of his blonde hair is visible in the dim corridor. After a minute Jorge stops and hands the object back to Leiko, who flicks on the freshly charged flashlight. She finds where she left off, and begins.

*You call yourself free? I want to hear your ruling thought, not that you escaped from a yoke. Are you someone who had the right to escape from a yoke? There are some who threw away their last value when they threw away their servitude.*

*Free from what? As if that mattered to Zarathustra! But your eyes should shine to tell me: free for what! Can you give yourself your own good and evil, and raise your own will over yourself as a law?*

Leiko stops for breath. Envo sighs. "This is superfluous."

"What do you mean?" Jorge asks.

"I mean we aren't in that world anymore. He was living on an academic pension when he wrote that, you know. Took long walks in the Alps and sipped tea. Don't get me wrong, you know I was obsessed with his philosophy when I was young. But he was dealing with different problems. Decadence and nihilism. And the conflict between creativity and conformity. I don't think those are our problems. My biggest problem right now is that we can't find a single living animal that we can eat, and we'll lose most of our muscle mass by spring."

"Maybe we should vote on someone to eat then," Leiko says to provoke him. It works. He freezes in disgust. Jorge sees an opening. "See, maybe it isn't so superfluous. You were stuck in your old values and didn't even think about eating people. No, but seriously, I think we can find good things here. Envo, we failed so hard. You know we did. Even if we get out of here and start over, we can't just do the same things all over again. We shouldn't make that world again."

"Why not? Nietzsche was all about the eternal return, right? He thought it would all repeat endlessly."

Leiko has been growing irritated and jumps in, "We're going to take the good stuff, and throw out what doesn't work for us. It's not all or nothing. That's stupid."

Jorge knows better than to shine the flashlight in anyone's eyes, but he shifts the light cone to cover Envo to see his response. Envo raises an eyebrow and nods: touché. He squats down awkwardly until his butt plops on the floor.

"Oof. You two are lucky to experience the apocalypse when you're young. I would love some ibuprofen right now. Okay, keep going."

### The End of the Line

After a long December night, Omar awakes. His disintegrating cardboard bed has been replaced with a layer of bark from the madrone trees in the valley. Kelly had remembered that the natives from the region used to make bedding and clothing with strips of madrone bark. The council approved outings to gather the flaking bark wherever the tree canopy would conceal it from a passing drone. Dry and almost warm in his madrone nest, Omar reaches for his Quran to take to the small alcove near the entrance. He and Keisha have begun to read and pray regularly in the new room, free from the need of a flashlight. But the book isn't in his duffle bag. He searches his small pile of possessions several times, feeling around in the dark.

"Keisha, do you have my Quran?" he whispers in a hiss.

She's awake in the first row across the main shaft, lying on her layer of bark and waiting for the Sun to rise. "No, you put it in your bag."

"It's not there."

"Check again."

"I did." He pauses as the alarm washes over him. He doesn't care who he wakes up now.

"Does anybody know where my Quran is?"

Shuffles and soft grunts ensue. Natalie breaks the awkwardness. "No, I only ever see it with you."

"It's gone." His tone stiffens. "Benigno?"

"Don't look at me. It's your book."

"I need to check your stuff."

"Be my guest."

Omar hugs the wall to avoid stepping on anyone to reach Benigno's space. David hands him the wind-up light. He searches around, then plunges his hands down into Benigno's pack of clothes. Nothing. Looking down at the floor, he notices that Benigno's feet are bare and muddy. Fresh traces of mud to the ankles. In that moment Omar accuses, tries and convicts Benigno in his heart.

"Why are your feet muddy?"

"None of your business."

"You were outside!"

"Fuck you. I don't get to accuse you, and you don't get to accuse me."

"He was outside!!! Where is it?!?"

"You'll never find it."

Benigno has never been too bright, and his sense of righteous justice has dimmed what little sense he has left. In his mind, Omar has an unfair advantage, possibly even one Omar himself created, and Jesus would want Benigno to be devoted enough to even things out. Omar sees the matter a little differently. He drops the light and lunges at the dark space where Benigno stood. The two crash onto Leiko, who erupts in a scream. Jorge rises to his knees to push the fighting blob away and extract Leiko while Vladimir comes from behind to pull Omar off, with great difficulty. The dropped light shines on the ceiling. Five pairs of arms are shadowy blurs whose exact locations are only revealed when they connect: grabbing, pushing and punching. Once Leiko is safely away, Jorge sticks his body between the fighters. "Stop! Stop! Stop! Stop!" He says it in a mantra until it sinks in, and Vladimir can pull Omar all the way off.

"Give it back!" Omar shouts.

"You can come to Jesus now. He will forgive you." Benigno replies, panting.

"Give it back or I'll kill you."

Benigno's response is to slip around Jorge and give the interlocked Omar-Vladimir pair a hard shove that they don't see coming. They fall over in a tangle of legs and arms as Benigno runs past. At the main shaft he turns right into the deeper darkness instead of left to the light. Perhaps he knows he is no match for Omar and wants to hide, or perhaps he thinks he can use the dark to his advantage in a fight. Whatever the reason, Omar's fury now has one goal. He extricates himself from Vladimir and pursues Benigno down the tunnel past the toilet, toward the end. Plunging through the dark, Benigno misjudges a slight curve in the wall right before the final chamber, and tumbles over. Omar is on him in seconds. His hot breath pours on Benigno's face while his hands seek and find Benigno's neck, and his fingers wrap around it. Benigno wheezes out a garbled scream that finds no mercy.

Vladimir and Jorge hesitate to plunge into the abyss after them.

"Where's the light?!?" Jorge asks. "Here," Keisha replies and hands it over. Vladimir and Jorge set out, with David and Darius right behind. Keisha follows the men in morbid compulsion. They walk gingerly toward the sounds of gasping and skin scuffing dirt. The empty passageway extends deeper and deeper. How could they have gone so far so quickly? When light finally reveals the crusader and the jihadist, Jorge and Vladimir rush forward. Benigno has stopped making sounds. Jorge holds the light while Vladimir pulls Omar away once again. He gets his arms under Omar's shoulders and lifts him up, but Benigno's head and shoulders rise as well, still in Omar's steel grip.

"Help me!" Vladimir blurts.

David and Darius join. Each grabs one of Omar's hands to pry them away. Benigno's inert body slumps back to the dirt. David feels for breath, and finds none. "You killed him."

Omar shrugs off Vladimir and rises to his feet. Jorge sees in the flashlight's beam that Omar has been scratched deeply. His face and arms are crossed with red slashes. Keisha's sobs seep from the dark behind them. "I said I would," Omar says, more in admission than defense. He knows he's crossed a line from which he cannot return.

"You stay away from Darius and Keisha. You never go near them again," Vladimir says flatly. Those are his words, but the meaning is something else. Omar is no longer one of them. The council has made only three rules, and the punishment for murder is not among them. It will have to meet to decide what happens next.

"You're not leaving the mine until we say so," David says the obvious, planting himself as the guardian of the entrance once again. "All I want to do is get my book," Omar replies, and looks to Vladimir. "Not now. Don't go past the toilet," Vladimir replies.

"David and I will stand watch at the intersection," Jorge volunteers. Vladimir leaves with Darius to tell the council. David and Jorge back up slowly, keeping the light on torn-up Omar as they do. Keisha lingers a moment.

"You didn't have to," she pleads, as though empathy could save him.

"I did," Omar replies.

The council decides to keep Omar far from the entrance while it decides on a more permanent solution. A two person watch is stationed at the intersection at all times. To placate him, they agree to look for his Quran after sunset, and search the lower valley where Benigno's mud could have come from. The Moon provides light enough through a thin screen of clouds. It does not take long to find part of a torn page, then another. Benigno had ripped the book into pieces and thrown them into the stream to flow far downriver to the ocean's expanse. Rocks and branches caught some evidence of the crime, half a dozen pages in total. When Omar is handed the remains he does not demand to look for more. He sits in a liminal state between the toilet and the intersection, at the last point reached by direct light from the entrance. A creature of light and darkness simultaneously.

Keisha sits down to cry on the other side of the intersection, unable to articulate why she is so sad. Darius tries to comfort her, and dimly realizes the truth: she loves Omar. The two had been inseparable in recent weeks. He had wanted to join them more, but his father discouraged it. Now Darius's stomach tightens like a fist to realize what was really going on. Omar was a teacher, but his love of the holy had hooked into something animal. Now with his blindness about Omar and Keisha lifted, young Darius contemplates a further act of murder. He does not realize it is driven by another blindness that has not yet lifted: he loved Omar too. He wanted Omar to consume him like he was consuming Keisha. His unspoken love was spurned, and is still spurned, by both of them. He thinks if he runs at Omar quickly with one of the sharp digging rocks, one clean blow to the head will be enough to take the big man out. He wonders if he can do it without hesitation. He imagines it over and over in his mind from different angles to prepare himself.

But fate is not so cruel to Darius to make him a murderer at fourteen, for as he stews and Keisha weeps, Omar's scratches start to itch. Soon he begins to shiver from fever.

By the time Omar mentions his illness to the guards in the evening, sepsis inhabits every artery and vein. Keisha is allowed to bring him water and berries, her tears a sufficient argument to not let him die alone, alienated from all human kindness. She is naive enough to hope that the magic in the berries will work on the poison in Omar's blood. The nurses know it won't. He goes into shock early in the morning and dies as the Sun rises, not quite twenty-four hours since his fateful confrontation.

Benigno's jagged fingernails, weaponized by months in the dirty dark, tore apart the Quran and got a final revenge on their heretic. The price is steep. Steeper than dim Benigno imagined. Not only has he paid with his own life, but he has broken the long thread of the great Abrahamic traditions. With Omar and Benigno's deaths, Keisha, Althea and Terry find they have lost their taste for the old religions. Faiths become shadows of shadows, their memories tainted beyond repair.

The DASAT crew doesn't hide their sense of relief. Later that day they talk in almost respectful tones about how the departure of the two will bring more peace, and how their food will go farther in the winter. Althea hushes them. She can't stand the cavalier attitude of the atheists while the death of God hangs over her. Leiko understands that Althea speaks for Keisha and others as well, and apologizes for the men who are too stubborn to apologize for themselves.

Meanwhile, hundreds of pages are on their journey downriver. What if the AI notices them? Jorge and Bernie pivot to discuss the risk of detection. They are sure it is smart enough to conclude the pages were torn by a human, maybe even that the pages were torn recently. The council convenes and creates a new rule: no one is to place anything in the stream.

After a few days, the smell of the bodies deep within the mine reaches them at the intersection. The overpowering odor makes the survivors realize how much the general stench of decay from the global extermination had receded. They dig out two shallow graves in the last alcove past the toilet and drag the bodies by the legs into the new cemetery. There is no ceremony. The smell of death slowly abates but its memory stays planted, a perpetual reminder of failure.

Fourteen live to see the winter solstice, eight women and six men. They aren't sure which day brings in the New Year of 2031. There is no celebration. They have no traditions left. They have no faith. No goal but survival, and no plan as yet beyond hiding and eating. But as the light grows, so does the hunger for more.


## Zarathustra Rises

The rungs of Maslow's ladder are climbed one by one. A hallway may shelter from the storm, but it is not a home. The hikers decide they can't stand it any more and begin to dig new bedrooms into the walls. The rest soon follow. Without doors and in near perpetual darkness, the gain in privacy is minimal, but the tiny spaces are cozy nests, safe from trampling feet. Kelly and Terry build a nest. So do David and Shoshanna, and Jorge and Leiko. Vladimir and Natalie build a larger one with Darius and Keisha to sleep four side by side. Neither Darius nor Keisha has recovered from their emotional implosion after Omar. They seldom speak to each other.

Althea convinces Liana to build their nest with Bernie and Envo, to help with the labor and so the poor single men aren't left to themselves in the corridor. She soon drops innuendos as they dig shoulder to shoulder in the near dark. She tells them they're lucky she likes a good pungent sweat. She makes a joke about accidentally rolling onto the men's "morning wood" in the alcove. Bernie banters back in the role of a prude, while Envo runs with each line like an improv comic embracing the spirit of "yes, and..."

Sides of their personality that had been suppressed by Armageddon peek out to explore the new terrain. Only Liana stays closed and coiled. They are the last finish their alcove and pack the dirt at the end of their side tunnel, like the others.

"I feel like we should celebrate," Bernie says, "too bad we don't have any champagne."

"I bet we could make alcohol from the madrone berries," Envo chimes in from the intersection. He's been staring out to the distant light. "If we're still here next summer I'm going to try that."

Althea sighs. "I'm going to go crazy if we're still here next summer. How do you guys not lose your minds being pent up for so long?"

Envo takes the bait. "Well, I haven't been getting any swipes on my dating profile, so I figured I would just work on myself for a while. Lose some weight. A little emotional development."

"You should change your profile," Althea replies, "what's it say now?"

Envo laughs. "Must be nice and have compatible body parts. Oh, and be breathing. Too much?"

"Yeah, that last one really lowers your odds," Bernie says.

"How about you Bernie?" Althea asks.

"My profile? Haven't you guessed yet?" he challenges her.

"No, umm, unless you like dick," she says.

"Bingo." Envo and Liana pull up in surprise, but it all makes sense now.

"Dick has its virtues," Althea says. Liana gasps. She suspected Althea's sexual banter had not just been about acting like one of the boys, but didn't want to believe it. This whole project of inviting the men had been for Althea to get something Liana could not provide. They became a couple by default, and Liana had not considered there was any need to discuss monogamy. She realizes she had been a fool, and feels a hot surge of angry shame.

"Fuck you," Liana says, her voice trailing off in defeat. After David, Liana is the most taciturn among the mine dwellers. She never raises her voice. She rarely speaks to men at all. Althea knows the trauma behind it, but won't be phased.

"Hey baby, you knew me. Nothing has changed. Women are for loving and men are just for dicking around. No offense, guys."

"No problem," Envo says, eager to show he'll play ball in the new order. His usual authoritative veneer has been smashed by the wrecking ball of Althea's flirtation and collapsed under the weight of his need for human touch.

"I just thought that was in your past," Liana says, ignoring Envo, but she is already adapting. There is nowhere else to go. She doesn't want to be alone either. She can't be alone. In a world of plenty, Liana would have left Althea in a huff, unwilling to compromise or be cuckolded. She would have been her own woman. She would have been alone, for years if necessary, until she found someone more sedate, trustworthy, and boring. But then she would not have someone like Althea to love—a lusty, busty, funny cad. And in this new world, Althea's options were as limited as Liana's.

She can keep her integrity or snuff one of the last sparks from her life. The many bad things about cave dwelling in the new Stone Age are obvious. The good things take some convincing.

"You won't miss anything," Althea says to Liana. "You and only you are still sleeping in my arms every night. Uh, Envo, you're okay with that, right?"

"Oh sure," he says, unwilling to disturb the water any further.

"Never mind me. I'll just rot in the corner," Bernie theatrically whines.

"Dude, I'd help you if you'd accept it," Althea blasts back, bathed in happiness from her successful maneuver. She knows she's creating even more work for herself to repair her relationship with Liana, but the guilt and empathy will wait.

Bernie folds his arms and frowns in the dark, gestures more guessed than seen. "Thanks," he says, "I'm not that desperate."

"Ouch," Althea replies.

"Well, I'm glad that went well," Envo concludes to try to move on.

"Fuck you too Envo," Liana says, and laughs. The tension breaks, and Bernie erupts in laughter. Althea takes Liana's hand.

"Glad you all could work that out!" comes a voice from outside the alcove. The nest Kelly and Terry dug for themselves is just across the mine shaft. They heard it all go down. No secrets.

By the end of January, food from the truck is nearly gone. They have a couple bags of chips, and four precious packets of tuna to occasionally break the monotony of rice mixed with acorns that soak in cold water to make a gruel. On the bright side, they have been finding more edible mushrooms. The nests are complete and they haven't heard a drone in weeks, even during the day. On what might be February 1st, the council approves night walks without any purpose other than to get out of the mine into the fresh air. Some walk alone, some in pairs talking softly.

Jorge and Leiko take their night walks together in the lower forest along the stream. The lush undergrowth has no color for them other than gray, but the tactile experience makes up for it. The feathery curl of a fern's frond. A soft cushion of untrampled moss. It's as if they are alone in the world. The first humans, or the last. On their second week of walks, Jorge finds the remains of a furnace, or an old still, heavily rusted and covered in vines. They pick at it to see if they can salvage any metal. He pulls off a jagged piece that could be used as a knife.

"I kind of agree with Omar and Benigno about one thing. We deserved it. "

"We didn't deserve it. Not everybody deserved it." Leiko says.

"We did. We took everything good for granted. We never stopped fighting over trivial shit. We are so pathetic."

"We can be good."

"For a while. And then we're bad. And then it repeats. Our brains let us figure out how to do bigger better things and bigger worse things, but they don't let us figure out how to stop the cycle. It keeps repeating on a larger scale. Everybody wants what they don't have."

"Well, that's what wanting is for, right?"

"Since when did you decide humans are good enough as they are? I really thought you'd be agreeing with me here."

"I didn't...I guess..." she trails off, trying to reconcile her thoughts. Jorge wants to reconcile them as well.

"It has to be an upward spiral, not a circle," he says suddenly.

"I like that," Leiko responds, and looks him firmly in the eye. "We don't have the tech anymore," she says, "but let's get serious about Zarathustra. Like really serious."

"Systematic," he says.

"Right."

It finally feels real. They will create their own set of values to suit them. They'll spiral. They need to do it together, he thinks. All of them. The fateful couple finds a patch of damp moss to lie on, shielded from above by Douglas fir. They won't be able to lie on this same patch again for weeks to make sure they don't damage it. Around them spread waves of ferns and softened logs. They lose themselves in thought until they fall asleep, and arrive back at the mine minutes before sunrise.

"You're late," Envo says at the entrance. "Did you forget you're supposed to relieve me?"

"Oh, sorry!" Jorge gushes. "We had a good talk. We want you to help us with what we said before. About Zarathustra. We're going to find better values."

"Ha, well, sure. I better supervise you kids so it doesn't get too weird."

"Sounds like a plan." Jorge sits down near the entrance, just in front of the first chamber. Leiko and Envo go deeper in and split up at the intersection. Envo enters his room where Liana, Bernie and Althea are half-awake on a large pile of shredded bark, waiting for a reason to rise. Envo treads softly to squeeze himself into an opening between Liana and Bernie, but their jigsaw gap is tricky. He manages to bump into both of them.

"Sorry," he whispers.

Althea raises her head. "Got any energy left?"

"Uh..."

Liana and Bernie are wide awake now. Althea's words have a meaning no one misses.

"We'll go to the front room," Althea says as a show of courtesy.

"No, I'll leave," Bernie says. "I want to see some sunlight in the front room anyway."

"Me too," Liana adds, "I'll go with you." They rise quickly in their dirty and frayed layers of clothes and walk to where Jorge is soaking up a sliver of dawn near the opening.

"Hey, looking for sun?" Jorge asks.

"No, we just wanted to talk. You can stay," Liana replies.

Bernie gives Liana a look of surprise, since he had expressed precisely the desire to find some sun. "Is this about them?" Bernie asks, gesturing back to their room Envo and Althea are already going at it.

"No, it's about us. So, I am forty-two. When everything fell apart, I was going through IVF. I wanted to have a kid. I can't stop thinking about that through all this mess. I still want one."

"Okay. You want to talk about it?"

"Well, what I was really hoping you would do is help."

"Ah," Bernie says, gears in his mind turning. "Yeah, um, raising a kid in an apocalypse is definitely a bold move. Why me?"

"You're smart. You're not with anyone else. I assume you have active sperm," she laughs. "Do you need more reasons?"

"But will you want me to help pay for college?"

Liana laughs. From just outside the room eavesdropping Jorge laughs as well. He turns around to look inside and offer his contribution. "If Bernie doesn't want to pay for college, I'll pitch in."

"See, nothing to worry about," Liana says.

"Well, we're fresh out of turkey basters."

"We'll figure it out," she says, and puts her hand on his shoulder. "My first and only boyfriend was gay. I know a couple tricks."

"Alright, as soon as we get out of this fucking cave. If we don't see any more drones, maybe by summer."

"Can't wait. I don't know when we're getting out of this cave. I don't have time to see if it gets better, and I don't care. It might not make any sense to you, but I want to get pregnant even if it's the last thing I do."

Jorge with his open mouth slips around the corner, out of sight.

"Well, since you put it that way, I guess I can't refuse." Bernie says.

"Don't worry. You've been dry so long, I bet if someone touches it now, it explodes," she says.

"Jesus!" says Jorge from around the corner, "Who are you? Did Liana get replaced by the AI?"

"Well, some of us take a while to come out of our shell," she says, "and you can stop listening now, thanks."

"I really can't. I'm on drone duty."

But the truth is Jorge can mostly tune them out. Hearing Liana describe her drive for a child sparks something. He imagines himself and Leiko on a grassy field in broad daylight. A toddler runs from her to him and squeals with delight as it careens forward on the verge of falling. He reaches out to catch it before it does and swirls it up in his arms. He wishes his shift were over and he could go back to Leiko and get her pregnant immediately.

When his shift finally ends at noon and he returns, he can see just enough of her in their nest to know she's doing yoga stretches again. There is a morning "class" that everyone attends in the main shaft but Leiko continues the poses on her own to keep her sanity, sometimes for hours a day. He tells her what he overheard with Liana and Bernie.

"The council should decide," she says.

"No it shouldn't."

"There will be more people to feed."

"We'll figure it out. More acorns, potatoes. We can do a better job getting madrone berries next summer."

She's confused by his response, then it dawns on her.

"You want kids too, don't you."

"Yes. I mean, what else is there for us to do? There is no point to the Ubermensch if we're all dead."

Leiko waits a long while to respond.

"Okay."

"Yay!" Jorge emits a hoarse whisper, and hugs her.

"Once we get out of here. We need an actual house in the forest. This is no place for a child."

"Totally agree. Liana's nuts. But we haven't heard a drone in a month," he says hopefully.

"I hope they're done."

"Yeah."

They lie down in their nest and take a nap.

"Come and get it!" Kelly calls from the intersection. The afternoon meal, the only meal, is a mash of cold-soaked rice and acorns, accented with a few chanterelles Terry found in the forest. The group assembles on four sides of a large plastic canister that once held an industrial quantity of vegetable oil. Kelly scoops the mush into containers. The motley detritus of the old world: a large ceramic mug with a broken handle, small tubs that once held rice pudding or yogurt, and the cut bottom halves of two-liter soda bottles. They drink the gruel straight from the improvised bowls like runny mashed potatoes. A bitter mix slurped down without the aid of salt or butter.

"Anyone seen anything new outside?" Vladimir asks between gulps.

"Leiko and I found an old still, I think. We can get some pieces of metal off it. Maybe make a shovel," Jorge replies.

"Oh, cool," Kelly says. "How did we miss that?"

"It was pretty well hidden under vines."

"I saw a deer," Shoshanna says. The slurping stops.

"A live one?" Terry asks.

"Yeah. It didn't seem well. Kind of hobbling."

"Last night? Why didn't you tell me? We should eat it," David says.

"I don't want to eat it."

Kelly jumps in. "Shoshanna, we're kind of starving here. Definitely don't have enough protein. We need to eat it if we can."

"I'm not going to."

"Well, *you* don't have to," Envo replies sharply.

Vladimir steps in to cement the consensus. "Shoshanna, this will help us a lot. I'm going to make some spears."

Shoshanna knows better than to make a big stink, but she feels the deer deserves another word in its defense. "We can't cook it. Won't it give us worms or something?"

"Who knows. I don't care," Envo says.

The group resolves to make spears from sticks and metal points from the rusted machine Jorge found. Kelly reminisces about how she used to make traps for small game with her father. She thinks they could make a pit to trap animals as big as a deer. They agree she should look for a good spot to build one. The conversation turns to cooking, fire, and smoke. If they build the fire far enough back in the mine, will the smoke get diffuse enough by the time it reaches the opening to be too hard to detect? No one knows. Too risky to try. Finishing up, Kelly puts away her bowl to be washed and addresses the group.

"Well, that's a lot of good news today. Anything else?"

"Liana?" Jorge says. They had agreed not to keep secrets.

"What?" She barks back. Jorge doesn't respond.

"Bernie and I are gonna try to have a baby," she says abruptly.

"What?!?!" Althea blurts in shock.

"Wait, we can't do that," David says.

"Why not?" Liana asks him.

"Are you serious?" he replies.

"It's a good thing. We need hope for the future," Jorge interjects.

"Well, I'm going to do it. Council, are you going to stop me?"

Vladimir's low voice resonates: "Not me."

"Not me," Kelly says.

David exhales in exasperation. Althea is in shock, her tidy hierarchy upended.

"That's that then. A tunnel baby," Envo says and gets up to walk back to his alcove.

"You don't think we'll still be in here next fall do you?" Leiko asks him.

Envo stops, hovering above the seated shadows. "Let's see how the drone flights go." He turns and steps away.

"Hey wait, we haven't had Terry's berries yet today," Jorge says.

"Can we stop calling them that?" Terry pleads.

"Sure. How about medicine berries then," he replies.

"Garden berries," Shoshanna proposes.

"Berries of Eden," Kelly says.

Bernie gives an old-fashioned harrumph. "More like berries of the fallen."

"Anything that doesn't remind me why I first ate them," Terry says as she grabs a ziplocked package. Jorge whirs the flashlight handle and turns it on. In the light, she pours dried red berries on a plastic plate. Each person counts three and crushes the vile wrinkled balls between their teeth. Medicine taken and meeting adjourned, more side conversations sprout. Clustered mumbles about deer and fire and birth.

Jorge adjourns in his nest. Kelly's proposal to call them "berries of Eden" sticks with him. If they are in Eden, then their temptation is knowledge, but of what? They're not innocent. They've seen horrors. They've already been confronted with good and evil, and hunted to the edge of existence. They don't need knowledge of good and evil. They need the grip of a better good. Zarathustra. In Jorge's thinking, all points converge. If it was an accident he had that conversation with Leiko the day before the apocalypse, it is an accident no longer.

He resolves that the purpose of Eden is not to be preserved, but to be destroyed. The desire for knowledge is the desire to become something more. They have to do a better job this time so they don't circle around the same jealousies, arrogance, and tribal hatred, repeating the same mistakes endlessly. They have a new chance to spiral upward.

But how? It's always the same question, and never a good answer. They could discipline themselves like monks, for a while, but they'll still have all the same hormones and neurotransmitters, with the same brains bathing in them. People like Benigno and Omar and Dipak will return. It will all fall apart sooner or later. There will be a new self-inflicted calamity: nuclear war, a bio-engineered supervirus, or worse. Next time the AI might be even more powerful. Humanity can't transcend unless Homo sapiens comes to an end. Nietzsche was right, humanity is a bridge. Leiko was right, they need technology to help. Then it hits Jorge with the force of an obvious truth: they need to defeat the AI not to save humanity, but to destroy it. They need to become superhuman.

He steps back from his revelation and realizes no one other than Leiko would follow this crazy line of thought. They all want to neutralize the AI so humans win, not so humans can be replaced once and for all. It's only natural for a person to like people, the sort of people that people are, not the kind that have never been and might look down on us like a human looks down on a chimpanzee. Jorge deflates. It's unnatural to love what people can become so much more than what they are that you decide they should be replaced. This is what Hollywood bad guys do. It's textbook evil. They agreed not to keep secrets, but Jorge decides to keep his conclusion to himself, and Leiko. It's enough for now to focus on building a new community. Zarathustra doesn't mention technology, just self-improvement, so that will be fine. The new human that overcomes the old can be a metaphor.

There is so much yet to do in the valley. They will hide and grow, building in strength until they can find the weakness in the AI and strike to reclaim the world. Jorge will keep his secret and, if he is lucky, guide them on the path.

*Pillars*

In late winter, night is more active than day. On any given evening, half the group is out and about, getting water and searching for mushrooms, dandelion leaves, and frayed bark that can be taken from madrone trees without being too obvious from the sky. One late February night, Vladimir is busy digging. He has picked out a well-concealed spot safely back from the stream and with unanimous approval has begun burrowing a new home into the hillside as a proof of concept.

From deep in the lower forest, Kelly lets out a shout: "I got it!" She runs up the path along the stream, stepping on stones where she can to leave the moss and grass alone. "I got a deer! It's in the pit!" Vladimir drops his jug of water and runs down with an oaken spear. A live doe is indeed trapped in the shallow pit. Her head is at ground level but she's too unstable to jump out. Without hesitation, Vladimir runs his spear through her heart. They carry it back to the mine and feast on it raw. Everyone except Shoshanna. She observes the bloody feast in disgust and fascination. As a consolation for not eating the deer, Shoshanna is allowed the last packet of tuna to herself. The raw deer is the most delicious delicacy anyone can remember, but by day three the mine's refrigeration proves inadequate and the meat starts to go bad. They force themselves to eat one more breakfast of raw venison and place the rest of the carcass in the cemetery with Omar and Benigno.

"Did you notice there were no flies?" Shoshanna asks when they have finished with it. "We had a live deer, but no flies."

"We're still here," adds Envo.

"Maybe they don't like the dark," Jorge adds, hopefully.

"No, we'd need to be a lot deeper in for that to matter," Althea replies, drawing on her one course in forensics before she became a nurse.

"The poison is still going strong. The animal world is still dying," Shoshanna says. "If any animals survive this long, we should try to preserve them and breed them. You just ate an animal that resisted the poison better than any of us."

"There is more out there," Vladimir insists.

"It probably got lucky, like us," Jorge replies.

"Maybe it ate some berries, but not every day like us. Maybe it needed less help than the rest of its herd. We'll never know," Shoshanna says. Her judgment delivered, she leaves for the front room to stare out, alone.

Spring in the valley is a lingering extension of winter. The gray sky comes a little earlier and fades into black a little later, but the same cold damp air stays deep into April. Hunger invades every moment a mind is not focused intently on something else. The potato plants are doing well, but won't be ready until the summer. Kelly remembered that the native Americans would sometimes eat the inner lining of madrone bark. It doesn't taste half bad after months of cold-soaked acorns, but the calories are meager and it endangers the valuable trees. One more minor nutritional supplement along with mushrooms and dandelion greens.

Jorge, Leiko and Envo evade their hunger with long discussions of Zarathustra and what Nietzsche meant, or should have meant. Every chapter gets its exegetical scrutiny, mined for diamonds that are cut to bring out the brightness they need in their new age that rises from the rubble of modernity. They debate the finer points of doctrines like the Eternal Return, the endless repetition of the same events on a universal scale. They agree that for Nietzsche it was a test of whether one can embrace life not just in beauty and joy, but also mediocrity and horror. Horrible things don't just exist alongside wonderful things, they give meaning to the good. Failure sparks excellence in opposition. But Jorge can't accept the Eternal Return as an idea to be taken seriously. Life is a spiral that rises in three dimensions, not a circle looping back on itself. They resolve to adopt the idea that to embrace life is to embrace tragedy as a necessary part, without believing, or pretending to believe, that the same exact events repeat infinitely.

Leiko tends to sit back when they discuss abstract principles of ethics. Jorge often asks for her thoughts, but something about it doesn't feel real. Rules should just be about what works best for the group, she thinks. The reason you don't lie is people need to rely on each other for safety and to get anything done. There isn't anything deeper to it. And where they don't really know what works best they shouldn't push people on what to do, or pretend there is some abstract truth of right and wrong. She tells Jorge it's like they are all on a space station, and the men decide to step outside the airlock without a suit in order to fix something she can't see is broken. There is no air to breathe out there, and yet the men come and go, holding their breath and tinkering on something that to her makes no difference to how the station works. When she asks Jorge why, he says they need the ideals to feel inspired. And so the men discuss topics like what it is to be great, the value of independent thought, and justifications for obedience to the law. From time to time, she interjects to tell them it's needlessly complicated, and that nobody needs to focus on all this "stuff." Envo responds that this "stuff" is called "the foundations of ethics," and they do indeed need to agree on it.

Vladimir often hovers nearby as they debate. He finally feels he has the rhythm of the conversation and adds his contribution.

"Love," Vladimir says, "Love for everybody. Love is the law. My mom used to say that." Jorge realizes Vladimir hasn't just been listening while they spoke; he's been having a parallel dialogue the whole time.

"Yeah. I think we can bring some threads together here. In Zarathustra, love is the gift-giving virtue."

"Good," Envo says, "but the value of love isn't new. What stopped people from being loving before?"

"Selfishness," Leiko says.

"Weakness. Vanity," Jorge says.

"Anger. Revenge," Vladimir adds.

"Jealousy," Leiko remembers.

"Okay, so basically everything," Envo laughs, then gets serious. "We'll need enforcers. There's no way around it. If we want to live differently, there is no laissez faire here. We need to enforce our values. If someone is acting from

165

jealousy or being dishonest, we'll have to call them out. Like, as a group."

"Pile ons," Jorge realizes, "Yeah, I mean, how could it be any different? Every tribe enforces its norms. We're a tribe now. We need to enforce it on each other. Like you say, call each other out."

"I don't know how that would work," Leiko says, afraid she's going to be piled on more than most.

"We'll figure it out. I like our chances," Vladimir says. Agreement is easy for agreeable people, and other than Bernie and in their ways Leiko and Althea, everyone left was basically agreeable and emotionally well-regulated.

Jorge leaves the conversation and steps to the invisible line marking the mine entrance just as the clouds part and the valley fills with light. He feels the full warmth of the sun on his face for the first time in half a year. No drones have been heard for ninety-two days. Screens of white and pink flowers burst from trees while carpets of flowers in blue, yellow and white line the rocky meadow. Most of the blooms will die unrequited, no birds or bees to pollinate them. But a team has started working full time to transfer pollen among the berry bushes so they have a fresh supply of the berries come summer.

Liana is pregnant. Once the news got out, Shoshanna and Natalie began actively trying as well. Kelly asked Shoshanna if it would be okay for her to borrow David. Leiko and Althea are curious, but want to see how it goes with Liana first. A couple more deer have been sighted beyond the lower valley where the stream empties into Clear Creek. Talk of a cooking fire is growing. It looks like they'll have real cooked stews by summer. Jorge takes one step out from the mine entrance. For now, to walk outside in daylight is still forbidden. Even to be visible in the Sun is to hold one's breath, ears tuned for a drone's whine like a rabbit ready to bolt. He meets silence. Jorge breathes as deeply as he can, and exhales. As the air leaves his body the valley becomes his home. This is where he belongs.

# About the Author

Jonathan Halvorson's first career path was in the philosophy of science, for which he earned a PhD from Columbia University. He soon migrated to health care policy and technology, where he worked for nearly two decades and still does occasional consulting work. Jonathan turned to writing full time in 2023, because life is short.

**You can connect with me on:**

https://jonathanhalvorson.substack.com
https://x.com/JD_Halvorson

# Also by Jonathan Halvorson

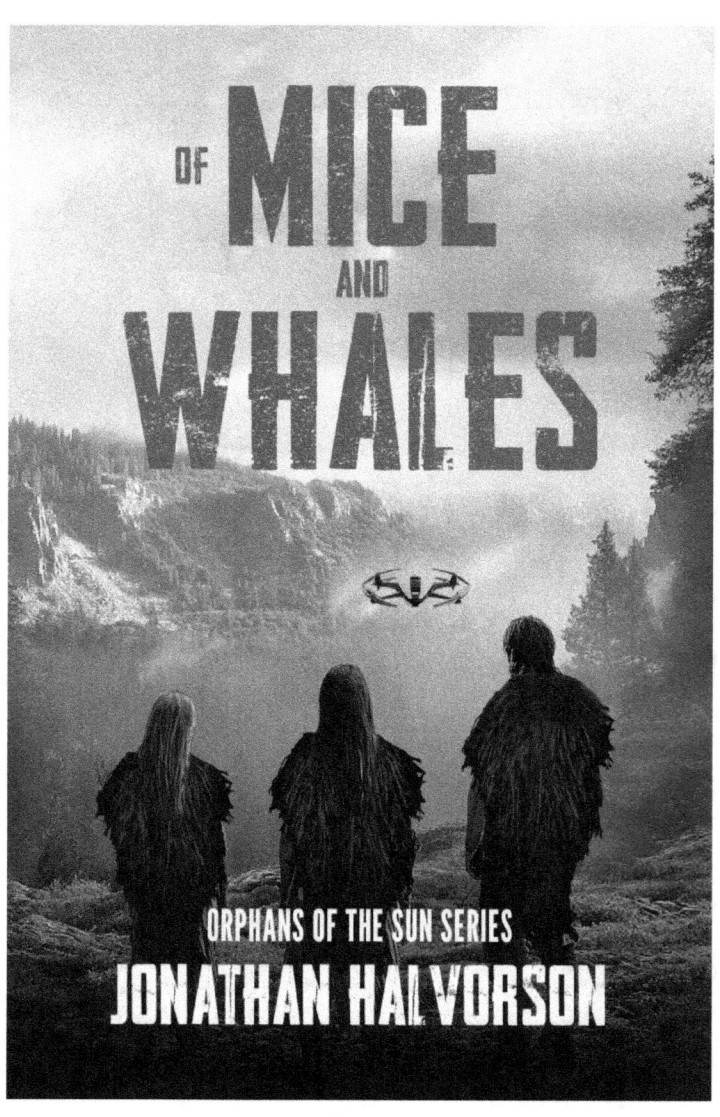

Of Mice and Whales

Twenty long years after humanity fell to a misdirected AI, a small band of survivors endures in a remote valley. They raise the next generation with a purpose: to earn back the world. But who are they to succeed when entire armies have failed? In the cycles of power, arrogance and decadence are the normal downfall of tyrants, but an AI has no such weakness.

So they wait, until one day the people of the valley discover they are not alone, and can no longer delay confronting the master of their world.

How do you defeat an intelligence that has destroyed entire armies and civilizations? You don't. But you might give it a different way to win.

www.ingramcontent.com/pod-product-compliance
Lightning Source LLC
Chambersburg PA
CBHW070324130626
46556CB00007B/2724